T0054145

Kyle Cassidy

JEFF VANDERMEER

The Strange Bird

Jeff VanderMeer is the author of the national best-sellers *Borne* and *The Southern Reach Trilogy*: *Annihilation*, *Authority*, and *Acceptance*. His novels have won the Nebula Award and the Shirley Jackson Award, and have been translated into thirty languages. His short fiction has appeared in the Library of America's *American Fantastic Tales* as well as on *Slate* and *Vulture*, while his nonfiction has appeared in the *Los Angeles Times*, *The New York Times*, and *The Atlantic* online. He has spoken about the environment and storytelling at the Guggenheim, DePaul University, and many other institutions. VanderMeer grew up in the Fiji Islands and now lives in Tallahassee, Florida, with his wife.

ALSO BY JEFF VANDERMEER

FICTION

Borne
Annihilation
Authority
Acceptance
Area X
The Book of Frog (stories)
Dradin, in Love
The Book of Lost Places (stories)
Veniss Underground
City of Saints and Madmen
Secret Life (stories)
Shriek: An Afterword
The Situation
Finch
The Third Bear (stories)

NONFICTION

Why Should I Cut Your Throat?
Booklife: Strategies and Survival Tips for the 21st-Century Writer
Monstrous Creatures
The Steampunk Bible (with S. J. Chambers)
Wonderbook: The Illustrated Guide to Creating Imaginative Fiction
The Steampunk User's Manual (with Desirina Boskovich)

THE STRANGE BIRD

JEFF VANDERMEER

MCD × FSG ORIGINALS NEW YORK

THE

A BORNE STORY

STRANGE BIRD

MCD × FSG Originals
Farrar, Straus and Giroux
175 Varick Street, New York 10014

Copyright © 2017 by VanderMeer Creative, Inc.
All rights reserved
Printed in the United States of America
Originally published as an e-book original in 2017 by MCD × FSG
    Originals
First paperback edition, 2018

Library of Congress Cataloging-in-Publication Data
Names: VanderMeer, Jeff, author.
Title: The strange bird : a Borne story / Jeff VanderMeer.
Description: First paperback edition. | New York : MCD / Farrar,
    Straus and Giroux, 2018. | "Originally published as an e-book
    original in 2017 by MCD × FSG Originals"—Title page verso.
Identifiers: LCCN 2017040458 | ISBN 9780374537920 (pbk.)
Subjects: GSAFD: Science fiction. | Fantasy fiction.
Classification: LCC PS3572.A4284 S77 2018 | DDC 813/.54—dc23
LC record available at https://lccn.loc.gov/2017040458

Designed by Abby Kagan

Our books may be purchased in bulk for promotional, educational, or
business use. Please contact your local bookseller or the Macmillan
Corporate and Premium Sales Department at 1-800-221-7945, exten-
sion 5442, or by e-mail at MacmillanSpecialMarkets@macmillan.com.

www.fsgoriginals.com • www.fsgbooks.com
Follow us on Twitter, Facebook, and Instagram at @fsgoriginals

10   9   8   7   6

FOR ANN

*Thanks to Sjón for allowing me to
borrow one of his blue foxes.*

THE STRANGE BIRD

THE ESCAPE

The Strange Bird's first thought was of a sky over an ocean she had never seen, in a place far from the fire-washed laboratory from which she emerged, cage smashed open but her wings, miraculous, unbroken. For a long time the Strange Bird did not know what sky really was as she flew down underground corridors in the dark, evading figures that shot at one another, did not even know that she sought a way out. There was just a door in a ceiling that opened and a scrabbling and scrambling with something ratlike after her, and in the end, she escaped, rose from the smoking remnants below. And even then she did not know that the sky was blue or what the sun was, because she had flown out into the cool night air and all her wonder resided in the points of light that blazed through the darkness above. But then the joy of flying overtook her and she went higher and higher and higher, and she did not care who saw or what awaited her in the bliss of the free fall and the glide and the limitless expanse.

Oh, for if this was life, then she had not yet been alive!

❧

The sunrise that blazed out from the horizon across the desert, against a wall of searing blue, blinded her and in her surprise made the Strange Bird drop from her perch on an old dead tree to the sands below.

For a time, the Strange Bird kept low to the ground, wings spread out, frightened of the sun. She could feel the heat of the sand, the itch of it, and sensed the lizards and snakes and worms and mice that lived down below. She made her way in fits and starts across the desert floor that had once been the bed of a vast sea, uncertain if she should rise for fear of being turned into an ember.

Was it near or far? Was it a searchlight from the laboratory, trying to find her? And still the sun rose and still she was wary and the air rippled and scorpions rustled out and a lunging thing upon a distant dune caught a little creature that hopped not far enough away and the air smelled like cinders and salt.

Am I in a dream? What would happen if I leapt up into the sky now? Should I?

Even as under the burning of the sun her wings seemed to grow stronger, not weaker, and her trailing passage grew bold, less like a broken wing and more like a willful choice. The pattern of her wing against the sand like a message she was writing to herself. So she would remember. But remember what?

The sound of the patter of paws kicking up sand threw the Strange Bird into a panic and she forgot her fear of the burning orb and flew off into the air, almost straight up, up, and up, and no injury came to her and the blue enveloped her and held her close. Circling back over her passage, against the wind, taxing the strength of her wings, she spotted the two foxes that had been sniffing her trail.

They looked up at her and yipped and wagged their tails. But the Strange Bird wasn't fooled. She dive-bombed them once, twice, for the fun of it, and watched them yelp with an injured look in their eyes, even though behind it lay a cold gleam and ravenous smiles.

Then she wheeled high again and, taking care not to stare directly into the sun, headed southeast. To the west lay the laboratory where they had done such beautiful, such terrible things.

Where was she headed, then?

Always to the east, always veering south, for there was a

compass in her head, an insistent compass, pushing her forward.

What did she hope for?

To find a purpose, and for kindness, which had not yet been shown to her.

Where did she wish to come to rest?

A place she could call home, a place that was safe. A place where there might be others of her kind.

THE DARK WINGS

The next day a vision of a city quavered and quivered on the horizon alongside the sun. The heat was so intense that the city would not stop moving through waves of light. It resembled hundreds of laboratories stacked atop and alongside each other, about to fall over and break open.

With a shudder, the Strange Bird veered to the southwest, then east again, and in a little while the mighty city melted into bands and circles of darkness against the sand, and then it vanished. Had the sun destroyed it? Had it been a kind of ghost? The word *ghost* felt gritty in her head, something unfamiliar, but she knew it meant an end to things.

Was the laboratory a ghost now? Not to her.

On the seventh day after the intruders had dug their way up into the laboratory . . . on that day, the scientists, cut off from supplies, and under siege in the room that held the artificial island meant only for their creations, had begun to slaughter the animals they had created, for food.

The Strange Bird had perched for safety on a hook near the ceiling and watched, knowing she might be next. The badger that stared up, wishing for wings. The goat. The monkey. She stared back at them and did not look away, because to look away was to be a coward and she was not cowardly. Because she must offer them some comfort, no matter how useless.

Everything added to her and everything taken away had led to that moment and from her perch she had radiated love for every animal she could not help, with nothing left over for any human being.

Not even in the parts of her that were human.

She encountered her first birds in the wild soon after she left the ghost city behind, before turning southeast again. Three large and dark birds that rode the slipstream far above her and, closer, a flock of tiny ones. She sang out her song to them, meant as friendly greeting, that recognized them as kin, that said although she did not know them, she loved them. But the little birds, with their dart-dots for eyes and the way they swarmed like a single living creature, rising up and falling down wavelike, or like a phantom shadow tumbling through the air, did not recognize her as kin. There was too much else inside her.

They treated the Strange Bird as foe, with a great raspy chirping, the beat of wings mighty as one, and raked at her with their beaks. She dropped and rolled, bewildered, to get below them, but they followed, pecking and making of their dislike a vast orchestral sound, and she wore a coat of them, felt their oily mottled feathers scraping against hers.

It was an unbearable sensation, and with a shriek the Strange Bird halted her dive and instead rose fast, tunneling up through a well of cold air, against the weight of her kin, until the little birds peeled off, could not follow that high, and became a cloud below, furious and gnatlike. While the cold wind brought her a metallic smell and the world opened up, so the Strange Bird could see on the curving edges that the desert did end, and on one corner at least turned green and wooded. A faint but sharp scent of sea salt tantalized, faded into nothing, but spoke to the compass within her, which came alive once again.

But now the three dark-winged monsters that had been above her drifted to either side, the feathers at the ends of wide wings like long fingers and their heads gray and bereft of feathers and their eyes tinged red.

They rode the wind in silence for several minutes, and the Strange Bird was content to recover in the dark wings' company. But a prickling of her senses soon became an alert that the dark wings were probing the edges of her mind, the defenses the scientists had placed there. Walls the Strange Bird hadn't known existed slid into place and, following certain protocols, a conduit opened while all else became a shield, sacrosanct.

Origin?

Purpose?

Destination?

Words that appeared in her head, placed there by the dark wings. She had no answer, but in approaching her, they had opened themselves up and because they were older, they had no sense yet of the danger, of how their own security had been breached by the complex mechanisms living inside the Strange Bird. Much of what was new in them, of their own making, had arisen solely to talk to each other with more autonomy, to become more like birds.

For the Strange Bird realized that, just like her, they were not strictly avian, and that unlike her, parts of them were not made of flesh at all. With a shock, she came to understand that, like living satellites, they had been circling the world for a vast amount of time, so many years she could barely hold them in her head. She saw that they were tasked with watching from above and transmitting information to a country that no longer existed, the receiving station destroyed long ago, for a war that had been over for even longer.

In their defenselessness, performing their old tasks, keeping data until full to bursting, erasing some of it, to begin again, the Strange Bird gleaned a view of the world that had been, saw cities cave in on themselves or explode outward like passionflower blooms opening, a tumbling and an expansion that was, at its heart, the same thing. Until there was just what observed from above, in the light and the dark, sentinel-silent and impartial, not inclined to judgment . . . for what would the judgment be? And how would a sentence be carried out now that all those responsible were dead and buried? But in these images, the Strange Bird knew that, perversely, the laboratory had functioned as sanctuary . . . just not for the animals kept there.

The dark wings needed no food. They needed no water. Ceaselessly they flew and ceaselessly they scanned the land beneath them, and never had their talons felt the firmness of a perch or their beaks food. The thought brought an almost human nausea to the Strange Bird.

Shall I set you free? she queried. And in a way, she meant to set the world within them free, too.

For she could see that this was possible, that with the right command, the dark wings would drop out of their orbits and think for themselves, in their way, and rejoin the landscape beneath them. What they would do then, she didn't know, but surely this would be a comfort to them?

But the query alarmed the dark wings, tripped some

internal security, lurching back online. All three gave out a mighty cry, and right there, beside her, they burst into specks of blackness that she could see were miniature versions of their larger selves and the specks dispersed into the thin air. The dark wings vanished as if never there and the Strange Bird's heartbeat quickened and she flew higher still as if she could escape what she had seen.

Whether in a day or a week, the specks would find each other and bind together again, slipping into the old, familiar pattern, and once more three dark wings would glide across the invisible skin of the world on their preordained routes, performing functions for masters long dead.

Yet even as specks roiled by the buffeting wind, the dark wings communicated with one another. The Strange Bird could hear them, mote speaking to mote, sharing intel about her. Telling what must be lies.

Analysis
>>Composition: Avian, overlaid with Homo sapiens, other terrestrial life-forms. Unstable mélange.
>>Mission critical uncertain; synapse control override inconsistent with blueprint of original design. Interference 100 percent certain.
>>Conclusion: Sleeper cells exist. Unknown origin and intent.
>>Action: Avoid a void a void a void!

At dusk, she found a perch atop the rusted hull of a ship that had foundered there in the desert half a hundred years before. She was tired. A sadness had come over her as she had let herself drift, watched the desert transform into mountains of rusted electronics, of ancient caravans calcified and fossilized into the dunes.

With the sadness had come the knowledge that the Strange Bird could be mighty—and that she was almost as large as the dark wings. That her feet ended in talons meant to rend, to slice, to tear. That her beak was sharp and curved. That she did not need food like other birds, or did not need it often, could go without. In that, she was more like the dark wings.

As nocturnal life crept out at the margins and the wind slowed and deepened, the scent of animal musk welled up strong, and with it a metallic aftertaste, by-product of centuries of pollution. Constantly, the Strange Bird's system purified itself of ghosts, of particles that could kill, all much smaller than a speck of dark wing.

The Strange Bird could see as she alighted there, in her newfound strength, the history of the place in her mind, it rising up as naturally as breathing. Below the ship were buried many others, in the sea of sand that had once been filled with salt water. Even that place, the depth of it, the detail, was almost too much to take in, the world overwhelming.

New things were rising in her, capabilities she didn't know she had. They flickered on and then sometimes flickered off, as if the laboratory had not quite been finished with her. If she tried, the Strange Bird could reach out across the rim of the world, could feel life pulsing in all directions, even if hidden, even if sometimes in distress or marginal.

She tried to sleep, in the half-awake way that the Strange Bird slept. For always there was an eye inside of her that was awake.

THE FIRST DREAM

In the dream, the Strange Bird sees a woman with black hair and brown skin peeling a piece of fruit, an apple, from the garden room, and cutting the pieces into pieces and putting them in a bowl. This woman she knows from the laboratory; her name is Sanji. The woman hands the bowl to another woman very much like Sanji but taller and with a rounder face, sitting on the couch next to her. She knows somehow that Sanji's friend used to work at the lab, but left long before the Strange Bird's own escape.

In front of them floats a moving image of other human beings talking and walking around. The women watch, joking and laughing. The Strange Bird can see the lab spreading out beyond them, still clean and new and fresh. The lights still work. There is still plentiful food.

Sanji feeds a piece of apple to her companion and says, "I save you from the bad apples. That's my job. All these years, I'm the only reason you have not died from eating bad fruit. I am all that lies between you and that fate."

The other woman laughs and squeezes her hand and a second name drops into the Strange Bird's head, but when she wakes she cannot remember the name.

Only a sense of peace. Only the crisp taste of the apple.

THE STORM

Headed ever southeast across the vast desert, the Strange Bird thought the world below looked so very old and so very worn, and only when she climbed to the right altitude could she pretend that it was beautiful.

The Strange Bird tried not to think of her dreams as she flew, for she could make no sense of them, hardly knew what a dream was, for it did not fit her internal lexicon and she had trouble holding in her head the idea of real and not-real.

Any more than did the prowling holograms that swirled up across the dead desert surface from time to time, performing subroutines from times so remote that nothing about them could be said to contain sense. Human figures welled up to walk, yet were composed of nothing but light. Sometimes they wore special contamination suits or astronaut suits. They trudged or they ran across the sands as if real, and then dissipated, and then came back into existence in the position where they had started, to again trudge or run, over and over.

Yet in watching this, the Strange Bird was reminded of the dream, and also of how detritus fell from her to the desert floor. Tiny bits of herself she did not need, and that she did not understand, for the way in which this material left her was too regular to be an accident, and she knew the compass inside her guided its distribution. Each time she regenerated the microscopic part that was lost so she could lose it once more.

In the laboratory, the scientists had taken samples from her weekly. She had lost something of herself every day. It was worse when they added something on, and then the Strange Bird had felt awkward, as if adjusting to an extra weight, and lurched off-balance on her perch, flapped her wings for hours until she felt settled again.

On the fifth day, just as the Strange Bird had become comfortable with this process—and the sun, the holograms, the cities, the higher elevations where the wind was so cold—a cloud blotted out the edge of the world, coming fast at her. She had not encountered a storm yet, but knew of storms, something inside of her programmed for evasion. But the cloud came at her too swift, too all-encompassing, and only at the last second did she see why: for it wasn't a cloud at all but a swarm of emerald beetles, and the chittering sound they made as they flew scared her.

She tried to dive for ground cover but misjudged the distance, and the swarm overtook her like a wall, and she slammed into it, lost control, fell through a thick squall of beetles, progress slowed by their carapaces, righted herself in time to—head down like a battering ram and eyes shut—push through them even as they tore at her feathers and ripped along her belly.

Breaking free of them on the other side meant a lightness that surprised, and she rose more quickly than expected, caught in a tidal pool of air created by their passage. Thought herself free—only to spy just ahead the reason for the beetles' panic: a real storm, spanning the horizon, and closing fast.

Emergency systems not triggered by the beetles switched on. A transparent sheath slid over her eyes and echolocation switched off so that she might rely on tracers and infrared in the midst of maelstrom.

Then the storm hit and she had nowhere to hide, no plan, no defenses, just the compass pulsing inside of her, and a body pummeled by winds gusting in all directions, trying only not to crash or be ripped to pieces.

The Strange Bird's strength failed her, and she tumbled, rose and fell only because the wind willed it. Perhaps she called out before something dark with weight spun toward her. Perhaps she made a sound that was a person's name as it struck her broadside, smashed her into a well of turbulence, knocked the consciousness from her. The Strange Bird could not remember later.

But whom could she have called for help? There was no one to help her, was there?

THE PRISON

When the Strange Bird regained consciousness, head ringing, she found herself in a converted prison cell in a building buried in the sand. Only the narrowest foot-long slit of window at the top near the ceiling revealed the presence of the sun. All was dark and all was hard—the bench set into the wall like a long, wide treasure chest was hard. The walls were hard. The black bars, reinforced with wire and planks of wood, so she could not slip out, were hard. No soft surface for relief. No hint of green or of any life to reassure her.

The smell that came to the Strange Bird was of death and decay and untold years of suffering, and the dim-lit view that spread out before her beyond the bars was of a long, low room filled with odd furniture. At the far end an arched doorway led into still more darkness.

The Strange Bird panicked, felt a formless dread. She was back in the laboratory. She could not find her way out. She would never truly see the sky again. Thrashed her wings and screeched and fell off the bench and onto the bare dirt floor and lay there beak open, wings spread out, trying to appear large and fearsome.

Then a light turned on and the gloom lifted and the Strange Bird saw her captor. The one she would come to think of as the Old Man.

He sat atop an overturned bucket next to a rotting desk and watched her, the rest of the long room still murky behind him.

"Beautiful," the Old Man said. "It is nice to have something beautiful here, in this place."

The Strange Bird remained silent, for she did not want her captor to know that she understood, nor that she could, when she wished, form human words, even if she did not understand all of those words. Instead, she squawked like a bird and flapped her wings like a bird, while the Old Man admired her. In all ways, she decided to be a bird in front of him. But always, too, she watched him.

The Old Man had become folded in on himself over time. He had brown skin but pink-white splotches on his arms and face, as if something had burned him long ago, tried to strip him away from himself. He had but one eye and this was why when he stared it was with such purpose and intensity. His beard had turned white and so he looked always as if drowning, a froth of sea-foam roiling across his chin, and with flecks of white across his burned nose and gaunt cheekbones. He wore thin robes or rags—who could tell which—and a belt to cinch from which hung tools and a long, flat rusted knife.

"I rescued you from the sands. You were buried there—just your head above. The storm had smashed you out of the sky. You are lucky I found you. The foxes and the weasels would have gotten to you. You would be in something's belly by now. A special meal."

The Old Man did not resemble a lab scientist to the Strange Bird and did not talk like a scientist, and his home was no laboratory the more she saw of it. She settled down, relaxed enough to search for injury, discovered soreness and strain but no broken bones. Feathers that had been lost but would grow back. She preened, checked for parasites, split two against the edge of her beak, while the man talked.

"My name is Abidugun. I was a carpenter like my father before me and his father. But now I have been many things. Now I am also a writer." He gestured to a typewriter, ancient, atop the rickety desk. To the Strange Bird it resembled a metal tortoise with its insides on the outside. "Now I am trying to get it all down. Everything must be put down on the paper. Everything. No exceptions."

The Old Man stared at the Strange Bird as if expecting a response but she had no response.

"I sleep in the cell when I don't have guests," the Old Man said. "The prison is all around us and below us—many levels. I was once a prisoner here, long ago, so I know. But that is ancient history. You don't want to know about that. No one does."

Although the prison was vast and the wind echoed through its many chambers during sandstorms, the Strange Bird would learn that all the Old Man's possessions existed in this long room, for it was where he chose to live and the rest was nothing but hauntings to him.

"I am the only one here," the Old Man said, "and I like it that way. But sometimes having guests is a good idea. You are my guest. Someday I will show you around the grounds here, if you are good. There are rules to being good that I will share."

Yet he never shared the rules, and the Strange Bird had already seen the three crosses that stood in the sand outside, which she thought were perches for other birds now long dead. She had seen the tiny garden and well next to the crosses, for she turned echolocation back on and cast out her senses like a dark net across a glittering sea to capture whatever lay outside her cell. The well and garden were both a risk, even disguised as abandoned, derelict, overgrown.

"I am Abidugun," he said again. "You I will call Isadora, for you are the most dazzling bird I have ever seen and you need a dazzling name."

So, for a time, the Strange Bird became Isadora and responded to the name as best she could—when the Old Man fed her scraps, when he decided to read her stories from books, tales incomprehensible to her. She decided that even as she plotted to escape, she would pretend to be a good pet.

But in the lab, the scientists had kept her in a special sort of light that mimicked sunlight and fed her in its way, and now that she had only the barest hint of any light, she felt the lack.

"You should eat more," the Old Man said, but the kind of food he brought often disgusted her.

"Life is difficult," the Old Man said. "Everyone says it is. But death is worse."

And he would laugh, for this was a common refrain, and the Strange Bird believed someone had said it to him and now he was under the spell of those words. Death is worse. Except she did not know anything of death but what she had seen in the laboratory. So she did not know if death was worse. She wished only that she might be that remote from the Earth and the humans who lived upon it. To glide above, to go where she wished without fear because she was too high up. To reduce humans again to the size she preferred: distant ghosts trudging and winking out to reappear again, looped and unimportant.

Beyond the dune that hid the Old Man lay a ruined city, vast and confusing and dangerous. Within that city moved the outlines of monstrous figures the Strange Bird could not interpret from afar, some that lived below the surface and some that strode across the broken places and still others that flew above.

Closer by, etched in the crosshairs of her extra perception . . . a fox, atop the dune, curious and compact and almost like a sentry watching the Old Man's position. Soon, others joined the fox and she glimpsed the edges of their intent and, intrigued, she would follow them using echolocation whenever she sensed them near, when there was nothing else to do, and for the first time she experienced the sensation of *boredom*, a word that had meant nothing in the laboratory for there had been nothing to test boredom against. But now she had the blue limitless sky to test it against, and she was already restless.

Her senses also quested down the many tunnels and levels of the prison when the Old Man went hunting, so she might test the bars, the planks of the wood, the wire in his absence. The Old Man often disappeared into the maze down below, with his machete, and hunted long, black weasel-like creatures that lived there. She listened to the distant squeals as he found them and murdered them, and she saw in her mind the bubbles and burrows that were their lives become smaller and smaller until they were not there at all.

How in their evasion and their chittering one to another did the Old Man not realize their intelligence? On the mornings when the Strange Bird woke to find the thin, limp bodies of the black weasels lying half-in, half-out of a massive pot on a table halfway across the room, she felt a sense of loss the Old Man could not share.

The Strange Bird knew, too, that the Old Man might find her beautiful, but should he ever be starving, he would murder her and pluck her dazzling feathers and cook her and eat her, like he would any animal.

She would lie half-in, half-out of the pot, limp and thoughtless, and she would no longer be Isadora but just a strange dead bird.

THE FOXES AT NIGHT

The foxes came out at dusk and peered in through the slit of the Strange Bird's cell at an angle where the Old Man could not see them. Their eyes glittered and they meant mischief, but not to her. They sang to the Strange Bird a song of the night, in subsonic growls and yips and barks. They were not afraid of the prison or of the Old Man, for they were not like most foxes, but more like the other animals she had known in the laboratory—alert in a specific way.

So she sang back silently to them, as a comfort, there in the cell, and when the moonlight lay thick and bright against the gritty cheek of the sand dune, the foxes would gambol and prance for the sheer delight of it and beckon her to join them, would let her into their minds that she might know what it was to gambol and to prance on those four legs, then these four legs, to see the world from a fox's level. It was almost like flying. Almost.

The Strange Bird knew that in those moments, the foxes could see into her mind, too. That the pulsing compass allowed this, attracted them. Yet as time passed, this fact did not concern her, for the freedom was too exhilarating and her prison too dank and terrible. In time, she wanted them to know her mind, for fear she might never be free, that they might take with them across the sands some small part of her.

Soon, she understood the foxes better than the human beings of the laboratory, or her captor the Old Man, and could call to them from across the sands and they would gather at the top of the dune and talk to her. Querulous, they would ask her questions about where she had come from and what it felt like to drift so far above the Earth. *Is*

that place better, where you came from? Would we like it?
Worse than your prison? How did you escape?

At night, too, parts of her still drifted off as they had before, through the slit of window in her cell, microscopic tufts that would leave her to become something else somewhere else. She could not know what it meant, what agreement her body had reached with the biologists in the lab that she had never said yes to.

But the foxes celebrated this leaving, for they would jump up in ecstasy at those moments, and snap in play with faux ferociousness at the microscopic things that left her, as if to herd them on their way, up into the sky, to drift and drift, and to never rest.

THE OLD MAN'S STORY

The Old Man never opened the cell door but only slid the horrible food in through an opening that he closed with a nailed plank of wood. He seemed to know that the Strange Bird might be able to escape through such a space and into the room without hurting herself.

As he shoved the food in, the Old Man always said, "You're good, Isadora. You're good, I can tell. You are beautiful and good."

But what was *good* and what was *beautiful* and why were these things important to the Old Man?

Nothing in the laboratory had seemed good to her, and *beautiful* was form without function. Anything that might be beautiful about her had a purpose. Anything that was good about her had a purpose, too. And still the compass pulsed within her and at times drove her frantic with the need to escape and thoughts of the dark wings, how they had disbanded and pulled apart and yet come back together.

The foxes had put the idea in her head—that she might escape by becoming a ghost. If she became a ghost, the Old Man could not see her and would think she had escaped and open the cell door so she could truly escape. The Strange Bird knew that the idea of *ghost* and *ghosting* meant something different to the foxes, but still she meant to try.

So she lay in the darkness at the foot of the metal bench, where the glimmer of sunlight could not reach, and she would grow very still and those neurons of her brain that lived natural in her feathers would alter her camouflage, dull the iridescence, practice matching the exact hues and tones of the prison cell. Her natural camouflage was meant to show dark from above and light from below while flying, so it took conscious effort to do otherwise.

All while the Old Man would talk to her about his memories of people and places she did not know and did not care about, and eventually mention the gloom and put on more lights, which meant taking slow-writhing white grubs that glowed and shoving them into divots taken out of the ceiling. By how he still complained of the gloom the Strange

Bird would count her progress in becoming less and less visible.

"My eyes must be going bad," the Old Man grumbled, but he could not afford to use more light, for the grubs would be food if the weasels grew more cunning, if his garden began to fail.

Then he would continue his sermon, as if a broken-down version of the chaplain in the laboratory, who would spend so much time in senseless talking to the animals.

"I am not the man I was. This place was different once. There are more people out there. All sorts of things out there. But I would not last without shelter. It takes some-one younger, stronger. Someone who isn't worn-out—and I know people will come here soon enough and wrest even this from me. And in the other direction there's just desert and wasteland and nothing good. You should know—you came from there. And this was the town I grew up in, al-though none of it is left. They're all dead now. Now it's just me and the lizards and the weasels and a toad or two. And sometimes an intruder. And now you."

The Old Man could mumble like this for hours, some-times rant and rave and become other than what Isadora thought he was. But even this the Strange Bird welcomed, for she understood him better and better through this rep-etition and she began to know not just his speech but his moods, to recognize the self-inflicted wound at the heart of him.

A favorite subject was of the city that lurked so near beyond the dune. Whenever the Old Man spoke of the city, his tone would grow hushed and his aspect fearful and the Strange Bird would remember the shadow of the monsters she had sensed.

"Best not to speak of that. Best to go on living and not think of it, either. Tend the well. Tend the garden, look not to the horizon."

From the city came guttural moans and roars, faint, and Isadora could tell that the Old Man could hear them, for even the most distant could make him shudder as he sat at his desk with the ancient typewriter, his back to her. Because he called her beauty distraction. Because he needed to peck away at what he said was his "great story." The story of his life and "how the world came to be this way, Isadora."

Yet she knew reports and stories from the lab, and she knew his could not be too great a story. For he had no typewriter ribbon left and only fifty sheets of paper and he counted on the stabbing imprint of the keys to make an impression like a branding, and when he had used the fifty sheets, front and back, he would start again, typing over what he had already impressed upon the page.

"For you see, beautiful one, my Isadora," he said, "it is a way of marking it all in my head. I type it to remember it, and if I never find more paper, still it is more real in my head and someday I shall get it down right, and forever."

But Isadora believed it was more that the typing helped

the Old Man forget the trauma of what he did not want to remember, for he stopped ever more often, racking his mind for details that she knew must have been buried in the impressions made on the paper and lost to him, except in the crisscrossing nonsense pattern of jumbled letters. If he could only leave everything there on the page, it could not live within him. She had no such outlet, and everything lived within her every moment, but she did not envy the Old Man his typing.

By the second week of her captivity, if the Old Man became too overwhelmed by his task, he would stop and talk to her instead, tell her what he had meant to tap out through the keys.

"Once, I had a birthday cake. Imagine it. I remember, age twelve, and I blew out all the candles and it was so sweet and moist and lovely and my face was sticky with it, because my brother smashed my face into it. I've never had a cake like it, and my friends were all there. Someone juggled oranges. I haven't seen an orange in so long. Or an apple, either."

A pause, a confusion in the single eye that stared so intent at Isadora. The flicker, the flutter of the eyelashes, the wince in the act that let Isadora know something within hurt the Old Man, something old but potent.

"No one understands anymore. It is all lost."

Yet what had been lost? The old world had been no better for the Strange Bird's kind than the new. Just different.

Then, said tentative by the Old Man, almost furtive: "If I let you out of your cell, you would stay with me? If I did that, you would stay, wouldn't you? If I trained you to stay?"

But she was silent and would not answer, because she knew the word *train* only from the lab, where it had meant pain and suffering, and because the Old Man had grown grim-looking and closed-off and in that mood he could be cruel.

So she only relaxed her camouflage, puffed out her feathers and turned more iridescent and allowed color to burn across the feathers like a wildfire, and as far as the Old Man was concerned, that was her answer.

That she was *beautiful*, and therefore *good*.

THE OLD MAN'S SECRET

One night, the Old Man came out of the tunnels into the room bearing a special treasure, as he called it.

"Alkie sardines, Isadora," he said, holding out a handful of tiny dry silver fish. "The Company makes these, or made them. I would have to go into the city to find them, but I stumbled on these down in the underground. Alongside a skeleton, yes, it is true, but he did not need them or any other thing."

The Company? She did not know what that meant, but

over time his mentions made her think of it as like her lab, but much larger.

He tossed a couple on the floor of her cell, held on to the rest, and then, giving her a big grin, shoved a half dozen into his mouth, crunched down on them, savored the taste, and swallowed them almost whole.

"Delicious, Isadora! Delicious. Try them. Try them now."

So Isadora did, surprised how little like fish they tasted, how much more like nectar, and by the liquid warmth that crept over her after they had disappeared down her gullet. Soon after, she felt as if floating and when she looked up the Old Man was hopping around in front of her and then twirling, arms held out as if hugging an invisible partner, and coming to a stop on flat feet to stare into the cell.

"Do you feel it? Do you, Isadora? This is good stuff. The best."

His one eye was bloodshot and the white on his face had turned deep red. He had a wild look to him, as if something inside was eager to get out.

But Isadora was too giddy to feel the danger of that, saw only that for once he seemed happy, and, in her way, she matched the Old Man step for step as he began to dance, flapping her wings as well, and hopping up onto the metal bench. Lost in the thought of dancing as another kind of flying.

Then, at some point, the Old Man got an idea into his head and stopped dancing long enough to haul over an old full-length mirror, cracked and worn. He held up the mirror to the Strange Bird, perched on her metal bed in the cell. Even with the bars and wire in the way, the Strange Bird could see her reflection.

It was the first time she had seen herself, her whole self, and what fascinated her was how color seeped and leached and spread and faded across her body even as she watched. How it fled across her feathers and welled up and that she could be so light in some places and so dark in others.

"You see, Isadora?" the Old Man said. "You see? How beautiful you are? Don't muffle that. Not in this world, so drab. Not in this world. You are like a blazing flame. A valuable flame."

Isadora the bird bobbed her head up and down.

"Good, good, good," the Old Man muttered, but she did not sense from him that her response was enough for him, or what response he had hoped for. He began to dance again, but Isadora did not join him this time.

When he became dizzy, the Old Man stopped dancing, while Isadora perched on the metal bench, waiting for the next thing. He held his head and slumped into his chair at the desk.

"You are a good friend, Isadora," he said, although she was no such thing. "You have made my life here better. Just looking at you has made it better."

He gave her a sharp glance. "Do you want to know who I named you after? Well, do you?"

He did not wait for a reaction but turned back to the desk, rummaged through a drawer, brought out a small metal circle, about two inches thick, set it on his knee, and pushed a button in the side.

To Isadora's delight—drunk for the first time, there in her cell—an image sprang up above the metal circle, of a woman, dancing, a woman in a dress, with a smile on her face.

"This is Isadora," the Old Man said. "I knew her, I knew her back then."

The woman spoke, just two sentences: "Oh, Charlie, this is silly, isn't it. Turn that off."

But he played it again, and then again. "Oh, Charlie, this is silly, isn't it. Turn that off. Oh, Charlie, this is silly, isn't it. Turn that off. Oh, Charlie, this is silly, isn't it. Turn that off."

Isadora the bird couldn't tell at first that the Old Man's expression had become grim, that he sat more stiffly each time he replayed the recording, could not interpret the emotion transforming his face.

"Oh, Charlie, this is silly, isn't it?" the Strange Bird said, in the same voice as the recording. She had learned the trick in the lab, where she had learned all else. It had pleased the scientists; she hoped it would please the Old Man.

The Old Man sat bolt upright in his seat, set the metal circle aside on the desk.

"Oh, Charlie, this is silly, isn't it?" the Strange Bird said, still in the woman's voice. "First we separate the surrounding tissue from the heart and lungs and then we gently insert the device into the side of the aorta. Then you will need to suction the blood away. Then you will need to suction the blood away."

"Shut up," the Old Man said. A vicious, scared look.

"They broke contain," the Strange Bird said. "They're in the compound. We'll be cut off. They'll slaughter us."

"I said shut up!"

"What choice do we have? If we don't kill them, we'll starve to death. It doesn't matter how distasteful it is, how much you hate it. How attached you are."

The Old Man threw the metal circle at the bars of the cell and shouted, "I said to be quiet! Be quiet right now!"

"And the bird," the Strange Bird continued, as if she could not help herself, but now was committed to relaying the last things she had heard in the lab before her escape, in the voice of the woman the Old Man had cared about. "And the bird can fend for itself. We have nothing to get at it with. So it will just stay up there, staring at us like a freak." They had run out of bullets. Had stared up at her with a hunger unlike the hunger of scientists. All except Sanji, who was busy opening the air duct.

But now she was silent, with the Old Man pressed up against the bars, his face a quivering mess, the one eye wide. She had shared with him and he had ignored her.

"You don't understand anything, Isadora," the Old Man said, weeping, and then he whispered his secret, in a hiss that promised damage, that foretold her own death.

It was not a secret Isadora the bird cared to know, nor did it surprise her. Nor did she understand all of it; she just knew that hearing it made her think again of the pot with the black weasels' limp bodies hanging half-in and half-out.

"If I must, I will kill you, Isadora, rather than be mocked by you. So you shut up. You must shut up and I must never hear that voice come out of you. Or I will kill you. Or I will leave you in that cell until you starve."

But Isadora the bird heard none of it, for he did not have to tell her that he might kill her. She knew. No, Isadora the bird was thinking of the lab and the night the animals had been lined up to play a game called chess in a corner of the vast blood room, one holiday when discord had pulled the scientists into separate factions.

Each tile part of the chessboard, ostriches for knights facing each other across the board, and lions and hyenas, porcupines and storks, even giant salamanders and mud-skippers, for the terrariums had yet to fail.

How the animals, as she watched from her perch on

Sanji's shoulder, stood so still and quiet, afraid they had been brought there to be slaughtered, for it was still the blood room. Sanji drunk, all of them drunk, or they would not have herded the animals down there, and all armed with guns or prod sticks, still drinking, some of them dancing as the Old Man had danced.

The way the staff had nudged the animals to move to play a game they did not understand, the roars of laughter that were also roars of desperation. How they did not know how to carry on, that soon, they knew, it would turn worse and worse still. Turning to the right in their cages, alongside their charges, turning right forever, because there was nowhere to go.

Was Sanji a prisoner of this, too? Were the scientists free to leave or not? And before the world caught up with them, would they finally discover what they sought in the flesh of their creations, and set free the animals and abandon the lab?

As she had watched what Sanji called *chess*, the Strange Bird knew that would not be the outcome. No matter what affection the scientists felt for their charges, it would not end that way. It would end in the blood room, the animals in their ranks, waiting for the end.

The Strange Bird had wondered at how she could think such thoughts, that she could be allowed such a rebellion, even if silent and only in her head.

THE SECOND DREAM

In the second dream, Sanji holds the apple in one hand, the knife in the other, while she walks down a beach in the shadow of stark cliffs, barefoot, in the surf. There is no one on the beach besides them. There is no one out to sea—no boats, no swimmers.

The Strange Bird walks beside Sanji. The Strange Bird is human but has no sense of her body; she might as well be molecules of air. The Strange Bird is overwhelmed by the sea salt and the rush of the waves and the wind that is both so strong and so gentle. The sand is cool and the lines of rocks half-submerged by the surf dark and covered in seaweed and limpets. Though she cannot see a sun, she knows that it is near dusk by the quality of the light. Though she cannot see a building, she knows there is another lab up on the cliffs, beyond the tree line.

For a long time they walk side by side, and Sanji looks only ahead and says nothing. The Strange Bird feels a compulsion to speak, but she cannot speak. She is still a bird. She is a bird. She is a bird. But she is human and walking beside Sanji, while up in the sky the real birds wheel and caw and search the sea for fish and other food. Some of them are not gulls or terns but albatross, and the Strange Bird knows that they have never felt the land beneath them, but have forever soared, and even as she watches they bank and then rise higher and higher until they leave their brethren behind.

"You will leave me for this place," Sanji says finally. "You will have to leave me someday, and then you will need to be smart and clever and brave. You will have to be very brave, if what we have done is to survive. And I will be brave with you. *We will find a way.*"

The Strange Bird wants to reply, has words to say, but she can say none of them, for when she looks down her body is not hers and she disappears up into the sky, as if ripped from the beach by an invisible hand from above.

THE ESCAPE

Isadora the bird chose a night to become a ghost that was already pitch-black, and she perched on the dark floor in the corner and she concentrated her thoughts and she tried to imagine she was not even there, and in aid of this she shut down all of her systems, her senses, all except sight and hearing, and she became so very quiet. And after a while she knew she had become invisible, that her atoms had become indistinguishable from the bars, the floor, the wooden blocks across the bars.

While the Old Man banged away at the typewriter, back to her.

She imagined that it would be a little like her escape

from the lab, and she was ready for that. The Old Man would be confused, would think she had escaped and open the door and she would fly out in a storm of wings, battering his face, and escape to the underground with the weasels. That she would, in time, find an air duct. That she would find her way to the surface and to the light.

Instead the Old Man finished his maniacal typing and tried to feast his gaze upon her, saw her nowhere, and shuffled to the cell bars, looming over her in the corner, and looked right through her.

A rheum of confusion spread across his features. A sense of loss, of unexpectedly fresh grief. But then he recovered, began to smile, and then to laugh.

"Ah, Isadora, you are a cheat. Why have you become such a cheat? You are all the same, in all your different ways. Each of you has a trick. There is a trick to you, but you're not as tricky as you think. You are not as tricky as I am. I know all the ways of prisoners. Do you think I have not seen this before?" And she thought of the three crosses in the sand. "I will not open the door. Oh, no, Isadora has flown the coop! No, I don't think so.

"And trying to trick me while I do such important work! After I have been so kind to you. Reveal yourself! Show me yourself! I will not open the door. Reveal yourself!"

His face had darkened and he was stamping around, punching the air. But she did not move, did not give herself away. Her plan had failed, but she at least did not want him to see her transform.

Then the Old Man said, in a clipped, hurt tone, "I could keep you here, but if something happened to me, you would be stuck. I do not like the thought. Would not want it done to me. Not to me. No matter how good or bad I was.

"So, I will give you a good home. A better home. Since you are so desperate to leave me. I will take you into the city and sell you. That is the best for everyone."

Was it best?

After a time, the Old Man calmed down and went to sleep. She could see him from the bench. He had lost weight that week and his beard was now so thick and messy that it looked like a nest. They had not been allowed nests, back in the lab, yet she knew *nest* in a way. His eye was more and more restless and sometimes his hands shook.

The foxes did not come that night. The moon did not come out. She lay in the darkness, exhausted, and felt the itch in her wings, the ache, how cramped the cell was, and so dull. It was, in a way, worse than the laboratory.

The Old Man's secret was still in her head, unspooling and respooling, never quite there, never quite gone.

The Strange Bird had not enough experience of human

beings to know which were rational and which were not. No one in the lab had been, in the end, rational.

THE CITY

The next day, the Old Man drugged her food and when she woke, she was no longer in her cell but in a sack, swung over the Old Man's shoulder. They were headed for the city. She sensed it was midafternoon.

Blind and bound, the Strange Bird jostled in the sack. The Old Man spared no thought for the jostling as he walked down the underground passage, through the maze of the prison. Cared not if she was bruised or harmed, and from this she knew she might as well be meat to be sold as a wonder to be marveled at. But she was not afraid, or at least not of the dark. For she could sense so many creatures all around: the lungfish hibernating in the floor beneath, the weasels in the walls, the salamanders in the ceiling, and spiders and worms everywhere. If she could not have control, then she would reach out and take comfort in everything that existed beyond the borders of her self.

Ahead, the Strange Bird could "see" the branches and pathways of the tunnel system, and discern which the Old Man might take and which he might not, thrilled at the danger when he came so close to some vast shape hidden behind a wall, a fellow traveler, shy and afraid of the light held by the Old Man. He had never known and would never know that he shared these dark places with such a thing, but the Strange Bird knew.

"Some secrets are between us," Sanji had said in the lab, in the evenings of those last days, when the other scientists were in their quarters or on sentry duty at the barricades. When Sanji would continue to work on the Strange Bird. Always with a local anesthetic, so the Strange Bird felt nothing, never became alarmed, but would be alert for these one-sided conversations. Why did Sanji want her to have the memory? She did not know. She just knew that confinement in the sack made those words come back to her, these moments when she could say nothing in return but must receive so much.

"Bird brains are almost as good as human brains—just packed tighter. But you're not just a bird brain, are you?"

Then what was she? If not "just" a bird?

※

The sky of late afternoon, and the Strange Bird pulled out of the sack, but swung by her legs, the Old Man wearing gloves for fear of her talons, and her working hard against the dizziness of being upside down, of seeing the arc of the rocky ground, cut through with rivers of sand come close only to recede, and reminded of a swing set, and how reminded? For that could not be her memory, nor Isadora's. That could only have come from the lab, from some other source. When had she been on a swing set? Everything dislodged, made into a pendulum, and glad only of the glimpse of the sun below her and then, on the upward swing, a bit more toward her, and then cut loose again, falling away again.

They had come out of a hole in the ground disguised by dusty canvas, crawled up onto the surface, the Old Man cursing, slapping her through the sack once, twice, as if it were the Strange Bird's fault, the discomfort of the journey, the length of it. But now the Strange Bird could tell, at the apex of the swing, that they were in the ruined city.

Soon, she would be sold. Soon, she would be elsewhere.

She held her wings close against the rope, stayed compact, preferred that ache to what might happen if she relaxed and her wings fell out of position. She knew the Old Man would not stop should she injure herself against stray rocks, which already she must avoid by moving her head from side to side.

The smell of this place struck the Strange Bird as unnatural. The metal, the rust, made her think of the flecks of dark wings, fading into swarm. The hint of tainted water and the funk of rotted flesh. Through lanes bounded by gaunt trees and yellowing bushes, with yellow grass, they crept, entering and exiting labyrinths of cracked girders and half-collapsed houses. Glimpses of tiny creatures shadowing, unsure if they were predator or prey, and her compass spinning wildly.

But there came as well tremors in the middle distance and a shuddering through the air and the Old Man spit to the side and picked up his pace. He stopped at the edge of a crumbling courtyard full of dirt and gravel and odd moss, bordered by four brick walls jagged and torn at as if by monsters.

"Not here, not here," he muttered. "Why are they not here?"

Surely it would be only a moment she would need—to plunge into the sky, to rise and escape and no longer be captive. That moment when he or someone must loosen the rope around her feet. Or could she break it? Could she tense and break the rope, or could she think herself strong enough to flap her wings and fly away even bound? Even weakened as she was by captivity.

Then, so that even the Strange Bird who had been Isadora could see it . . . a shadow appeared along the edge of the world, view constrained by the courtyard and the ruins beyond, something enormous launched in flight, seen indistinct. It could not be a bird by the shape. It could not be anything that the Strange Bird had ever seen fly.

There had been a bear in the laboratory. Patchy, small, inward-staring, even as it turned to the right to pace along the glass wall of its cage, and kept turning right and right again, for there was nowhere to go. She did not know what had happened to that bear, where it might have fled when the lab began to burn, how it would have survived in the desert. But the Strange Bird knew that this was a different species, a different kind of bear.

For this bear could *fly*, just like her, and although the Strange Bird saw him only from a distance, and wrong-side up, she could not breathe in the moment for the miracle of him. The way the bear infernal was also the bear eternal, a kind of angel or something that was unexpected and wondrous yet terrible, too, and every one of her many senses became overloaded with the information generated by that hovering form so far away across the skyline. Had the beast landed beside her, it would have stood four or five stories tall. Yet it dove and swooped like a swift or swallow catching insects, to what purpose she could not tell.

She did not care that the bear might be death; instead, her spirits soared because the bear flew, and suddenly she could imagine being powerful in her flight, so powerful that others might fear her.

The sight filled the Old Man with terror, and he loosened his grip on her and did not quite regain it, yet still she waited, for it was not enough.

As if the Old Man was ashamed of his fear, he scowled and stared down at her, that eye like a hole in his face through which she ought to be able to see the sky.

"That is Mord, the great bear. Company made. Company bought. Just Mord. No other name. He is seen here and sees you every day here, Isadora. Our curse, but distant. Not coming here now. He may be mighty, but he is also ordinary, no less ordinary than that abandoned sofa over there." Pointing to something long and soft with wooden legs that had been burned by fire and submerged in scalded brick.

But as he said it, the Old Man shivered and winced and the Strange Bird, even swinging upside down and tied up and held rough in his grip, did not believe him. The Old Man did not understand Mord, any more than he understood the Strange Bird, and that is why he cursed at his Isadora now and gave quicker glances from side to side, even as he must inexorably, almost against his will, check the horizon to make sure Mord stayed distant.

But the real danger was much closer.

An opening yawned from the ground above the Strange Bird's head. An arm erupted from the ground behind the Old Man, a hand latched onto the Old Man's ankle, yanked, and he fell, the Strange Bird sent sprawling and squawking. The ties at her talons loosened, there, in the dirt, and finally right-side up, she clawed them off, rolling to free her wings.

A trapdoor, hidden as the Old Man's tunnel entrance had been hidden.

A little man in dusty clothes and with a face like a bat pulled the Old Man toward him, into his lair, as the Old

Man cried out and grasped for the Strange Bird's wing, caught hold, so that as the Old Man was receding into the trap, he was taking the Strange Bird with him.

In a panic, she slashed his hand with her talons, pecked with the point of her beak. The Old Man shrieked but held on and as she pulled her wing away and raked him again, she could feel something in her give, something in the bone not meant to bend in that way.

She fluttered away, hopping, to the middle of the courtyard, turned back on one foot, still tangled in the rope, beak finally unbound, to see the Old Man half-in, half-out of the trapdoor, clawing the ground to stop himself from being pulled in. The little man with the bat face could not be seen but must be tugging at him from the other end.

"Isadora!" the Old Man pleaded. "Isadora!"

He reached out toward her as if they had been friends instead of captor and captive. As if she could somehow rescue him.

There came a great tug from beneath the earth, and the Old Man vanished into the trapdoor maw up to his chest. The look on his face, beard filthy with dust, was no different than that of a frog half-swallowed by a snake. Panic, perhaps, but also a kind of stoic resignation.

"Isadora," the Old Man said. "Isadora. Isadora."

Even though they both knew he was already dead.

Hurt wing held at an angle, the Strange Bird tested it

with a flap, aware that any creature watching might jump out and grab her, and took to the air, the wing inflamed, painful.

From the air, the Old Man looked as if he had never been anything but a head, a neck, and a chest jutting out of the ground. Waving one hand, staring up at her as she climbed, shouting the name that was not her name. In shock. In horror. While the bat-faced man worked on him from below.

Soon, the Old Man was just a dot below, inconsequential. Human beings had such strange ideas about gratitude. When it should be given. When it should be withheld. Should she be grateful for being imprisoned? What should she feel now? She sang out the question that was its own answer.

As she rose she could feel the name *Isadora* falling away from her, and she was just and always and forever the Strange Bird, who had no need of a name, not in the way human beings liked to name things.

THE BAT-FACED MAN

The compass within chided her, told her she must head southeast, leave the city, but as she tried to change direction, circled back around over the courtyard, the pain flared up in her wing and she realized she was injured much worse than she had thought.

The wing failed, would only stay extended, rigid, as it throbbed, and she could not control altitude or maintain speed. Below still lay the courtyard and to all sides unfamiliar territory, and no cover. Flapping her good wing, she made for a clump of trees on the far side of the courtyard. Spinning, drifting like a dead leaf, struggling again, the Strange Bird managed a rough landing—cried out as the injured wing smashed into a knoll, then swung herself right-side up with a tight grip on a blackened branch, hopped without pause into the midst of the thicket of branches at the center of the copse.

There, overheated and in stinging agony, the Strange Bird held out her hurt wing and surveyed the courtyard. She could see neither the Old Man nor the man with the bat face who had attacked them. Not even the trapdoor. But she did not trust the silence, the lack of motion. If she could not fly, then she must at some point hop and flap across open ground to other shelter, to a place she could recover and heal. A place with water. A cool, dark place.

What if the bat-faced man still lay within his trap, waiting? What if there were others?

She clung to the branch until dusk, too afraid to move. She would be patient. She would make sure.

When the moon came out, two large lizards came out with it from opposite sides of the courtyard, looked around with caution, then raced across the debris to the middle, chasing each other, as if the moon had driven them mad. But no predator pounced and when their giddiness had passed, they with a kind of flaunt separated again and headed back to sanctuary.

The one that scuttled past the Strange Bird's sanctuary suffered no harm. The other passed the edge of the trapdoor—and the little man rose up from hiding and, with an agility that shocked her, plucked the lizard from the ground in mid-run and stuffed it greedily in his mouth, and then knelt there, in the moonlight, looking around almost proudly, crunching down as the tail wriggled frantic in the corner of his mouth.

After that, the Strange Bird remained alert for a long time, but she must have fallen asleep, for she woke with a start to find the moon was still out.

The top half of the Old Man's body now lay crumpled and discarded against the far wall, his one dead eye staring up at the heavens.

She heard a rustle, looked down, almost lost her grip on the branch.

The bat-faced man stood beneath her tree. His face resembled a gray mask, glistening dark in the moonlight. Perhaps it was just a trick of perspective, the way the light hit his face, but the bat-faced man seemed to be silently crying. This creature that had killed the Old Man. This creature that had gobbled up the lizard.

He stared up at her with huge, scared-looking eyes, expression fixed by the immobility of a face with great flared nostrils and cheekbones cut at alien angles, all of it framed and seeded with gossamer soft fur. She could not stop looking at him, trapped there, even though he was grotesque.

Perhaps he didn't see her. Perhaps he would return to his underground coffin.

But with a hiss, the bat-faced man leapt onto the trunk of the largest dead tree. With great lunges and deft little motions to navigate around branches, the bat-faced man scuttled up toward her, and she was racing, injured wing on fire, to the next tree and the next, struggling to reach a place where his weight would not support him and where she might safely drop to the wall below, and then out into the city.

She felt the bat-faced man behind her, heard his hissing breath, made it to the wall, fluttered heavy over it and out into the darkness.

While still he sought her in the trees above.

The Strange Bird muted her feather color to a dusty gray and used the shelter of a drainage ditch to keep low. She could form no impression of the city because the city would not give itself up to her. It was too vast and jumbled and she was too distracted monitoring the heat signatures of life all around her to know what else to avoid. Sight helped her less than seeing the blueprint of the rubble, the hints of water vapor that led her to this oily puddle, to that collection of dew in the bottom of a ripped-open tin can.

Toward dawn, she was still lost in the city, did not think she would ever be free. It was too blank and yet so full of danger that she trembled from the effort of being alert every moment.

She had come to the corner of a bridge collapsed into the dirt and the remains of some failed fortifications, a low wall against which slumped the leathery remains of animals and rusted gun parts. Which way should she go next?

The man with the bat face appeared on the bridge, staring down at her. Impassive. Curious. As if she were a lizard to be gobbled up. Or worse.

He could sense her despite the camouflage, would always be able to sense her.

She panicked, took to the air despite her wing, shrieked in distress as fire burned through the join between wing and body, but rose awkward anyway, doing more damage spinning some small way up into the air.

The bat-faced man scuttled toward her, making his hissing cry, his features writhing and repulsive in the shadows.

The Strange Bird spread the wing full in a desperate attempt to glide, but fell back down to earth.

Then he was upon her and there was no safe place, in the air or on the earth. There was no escape. Her talons were not enough.

THE OBSERVATORY

Worlds spun above the Strange Bird and stars—stars so close, across purpling heavens, streaked with the light of far-distant galaxies and the dark intensity of nebulae, streaked with the gray light of dawn that crept in through cracks in the dome. To the side, the burnt umber rust of the great telescope that had once taken center stage, now tossed aside by a long-lost cataclysm.

A blue fox head glowed from the slanted side wall. Though it must be dead, a trophy, the eyes stared at her and the mouth moved to yip, the sound drowned by the voices of the others in that place, and so for a time, to gather herself, to not be afraid, she ignored all but that ceiling and the fox head, which was luminous even against the irides-cent paint used to create the cosmos beyond.

For the Strange Bird lay pinned and splayed out on a stone table beneath that horizon limitless that she would come to know later was the city's abandoned observatory.

In the backdrop, the blue fox. In the foreground, two faces staring down at her, framed by the cosmos, one batlike and familiar, the other a woman the Strange Bird did not know.

"What have you brought me, Charlie X?" the woman asked.

"Thing. Creature. Beast. Bird."

Charlie X always sounded like a nervous man in the

process of swallowing a lizard, kept his sentences simple so he could be understood. The Strange Bird would become used to him in time. She would understand that the set mask of his features hid a complexity of emotion unconstrained by logic or reason or even, at times, an instinct for self-preservation. That he could be kind, cruel, heroic, and cowardly all in the same instant, and in the instant after that forget all he had done. Perhaps it was best he forgot so easily, given he ate so much he should not eat. He called the woman the Magician.

"Kill them all. Kill them all," the Strange Bird called out. "Kill them kill them." She had only words from the lab with which to attack, to defend. She knew it was not enough.

Charlie X flinched, but the Magician did not move, nor did the calm expression on her face change by any degree, no matter how small.

"A *made* bird," the Magician said. "A sad, unlucky lab bird that never existed before. That somehow escaped and knows nothing of the world. I can tell."

"Valuable," Charlie X said, nostrils flexing. Charlie X's throat bulged and sobbed with something living housed within.

Around the edges of the stone table now crept a row of faces, the faces of children, until they surrounded every side, pushed up against the Magician, who paid them no mind.

"Soon, we'll find what you're made of, and then we'll have a show, won't we?"

The children all nodded at once and stared with shining eyes at the Strange Bird.

Something crumpled inside of her. If only she had not encountered the storm. If only she had placated the Old Man and not been brought to the city. If only the Old Man had not been ambushed. If only he had not reached out and caught her wing . . .

The Magician had pulled a spider from a pocket and set it to crawl across the Strange Bird. A long-legged crystalline spider that seemed to glide across her body, to fall into it and then come out again, while she itched, felt intruders within, slipping through locked doors. She could not stop that, either. Her security had been made by Sanji, and others who had a formal training that this eccentric, patchwork magic did not recognize or respect. This thing testing her, crawling over her, was wild, half-feral in intent. It scorned subroutines and extra senses. It was not the spider, she realized, but the will behind it—the Magician. For it was the Magician crawling through her brain while she lay there, defenseless. The Magician who would know everything.

The Strange Bird shut down as much as she could, was scrambling to lock more doors as the spider's probes approached, inexorable. But there were only so many doors.

More of her was leaving even as the spider encroached, like lifeboats leaving a sinking ship, and the ship itself dissolving, something Sanji must have meant to happen. Dark wings becoming swarm. The bits that floated from her as she flew; now they floated with more vigor, more intensity, more, more, more. Perhaps before the Magician could kill her, most of her would be gone anyway, motes that would float up through the cracks in the dome and out into the city.

"Be brave," Sanji said to her, a ghost, a firing neuron, a nothing. "And sometimes being brave means doing nothing, means waiting."

Still the children leered and Charlie X and the Magician peered down from an ever greater height and the spider delicate and deadly continued in its task.

THE THIRD DREAM

In the third dream, the Strange Bird is a glowing red apple on a stainless steel laboratory table. Sanji stares down at her in a lab coat and gloves and puts a finger to her mouth.

"Shhh—this is a secret between us. You cannot tell anyone."

But whom would she tell?

Then Sanji uses a scalpel to cut the apple into fourths. Seeds fall out of the Strange Bird's core and spin to the edge of the table and then over onto the floor.

As she labors, Sanji says, "You know, we met because of birds, because we both worked with birds. Not this work—I never wanted to work with birds in this way. But I had no choice, and neither did she. You should know that." The woman who used to work in the lab, the woman Sanji loved.

The Strange Bird feels no pain, no horror, at the incisions, feels instead a kind of relief, as if some tension inside has been resolved. Seeds should be on the outside. Seeds should fall away from the body and be replenished.

"There," Sanji says. "It's done. All you need to do now is go home. *Find her because I cannot.*"

With that the four pieces of apple take wing and each of them is her and all of them are the Strange Bird. They come together above the table and form a compass.

"The compass is the heart of you. The compass is at the heart of you. I've hidden it deep, and whatever else you give up, you must never give this up."

Except it is not Sanji's voice that says these last words before the dream ends, but some stranger's.

Then there is laughter, the laughter of two people sharing something clever or true, and the sound is melodic and cheerful yet so very far away.

THE TRANSFORMATION

The Old Man had told the Strange Bird he had lied to her because she was so beautiful. He had lied to her about the prison and his place in it. He had lied to her about the story he typed out on his typewriter.

"I was the jailer in this place. When the world fell apart, when there was no more rule of law, we went into lockdown. I left the prisoners in their cells. They would have killed me. Until they had starved to death. Then I survived by killing the other guards as they tried to kill me—and that is how I lost my eye and how I came to be burned. Until I was the only one here, talking to myself. Because that is the world we live in now, so I was only doing what I had to do, what anyone would do. Isadora."

What the Old Man had tried to capture, to remember, on his blank typed pages were the lives of the prisoners and the guards, to remember as many details as he could, so that somehow they might not be as dead. Which is how the Strange Bird knew the Old Man was not rational, one of the many reasons, but also how she knew that he could experience guilt, could understand regret, could want absolution.

In the lab, so many of the scientists had said "forgive me" or "I am so sorry" before doing something irrevocable to the animals in their cages. Because they felt they had the right. Because the situation was extreme and the world was dying. So they had gone on doing the same things that had destroyed the world, to save it. Even a Strange Bird perched on a palm tree on an artificial island with a moat full of hungry crocodiles below could understand the problem with that logic.

But the Strange Bird knew there was nothing rational at all about the Magician's spider, for even as it revealed her, it revealed the Magician to the Strange Bird, and this was how she knew to expect the worst.

The spider withdrew, the children—most of them naked, faces smudged with caked blood and grime—turned to the Magician, expectant, as if she might reveal some great truth. Even Charlie X looked to her as if she were a queen.

"Full of animals," the Magician said, musing, thoughtful, pushing the children away from her, sending a rippling wave out to the sides as packed so tight they fought to keep their balance. "Not of the Company. Not this type of workmanship. It has a specialized feel to it. Is their lab in the city? No, I doubt it. I would know. Where? Never fear—I will get it out of you." Now peering down at the Strange Bird again, addressing her. "And also what is staring out from your eyes. Because someone is. Someone not you."

"Can I. Can I."

"No, you can't, Charlie X. No matter what you might want to say."

"Reward. Is reward."

"Is reward?" The Magician laughed, a mocking laugh that even the Strange Bird, still struggling on the table, knew was a warning.

"Bird invisible. Bird invisible in tree. Charlie X see. Bird escape. But Charlie X follow, though, track down. Bring. Reward?"

The Magician turned in a graceful arc to face Charlie X,

arm extended, and when she stood motionless once more Charlie X's throat had been slit with a knife hidden in her sleeve.

Charlie X reeled, caught his balance, hand reflexively at his neck.

The moon-faced children, the sad, malnourished children, gasped and chattered in a language the Strange Bird did not know, or perhaps it was nonsense, gibberish. But they did not draw back or seem overly surprised and by this the Strange Bird knew the Magician was often murderous.

No blood came from Charlie X's throat and instead out poured a stream of tiny mice and she saw that the mice had already begun to stitch up the cut with their teeth, from the inside out, as the man gurgled and struggled to right himself, stumbled against the side of the stone table, hand as it met the stone touching her wing as well.

"Mind your place, Charlie X. Mind you recognize this is no apprenticeship. You bring me things. You receive favors for those things—for example, I let you live like a trapdoor spider in your courtyard kingdom and do not disturb you there. But that is all. You are not one of mine."

Charlie X had moved past caring about lectures and rewards, although the wound was now sutured and the mice returning to their lair, through his mouth.

"You are not one of mine." The Magician gestured to the children. "You are not young enough, and you are part Chiropteran."

"Am still young," Charlie X countered, amid a gurgle, but could not rebut the second thing.

But she snapped her fingers and the children converged on him, still intent on his own reconstruction, and dragged him up, struggling, and carried him out like a living coffin, above their heads, on their shoulders. A sea of children headed out of the observatory through the far archway, jettisoning Charlie X that he might return to his trapdoor and feed once more on the remains of the Old Man.

Surely, the Strange Bird had believed, there could be no place worse than the laboratory or the Old Man's cell, yet for all the beauty and mystery of the planets revolving there above her, the Strange Bird knew that she was in what Sanji had called "a kind of hell."

While the blue fox head on the wall stared down impassive, glowed like a lamp because the Magician had turned it into a lamp, but not given it the mercy of forgetting what it had become, and as the Strange Bird looked up at the still-living fox, she realized the Magician would not kill her. It would be worse than that.

※

The blur, the disassembly, the knowledge, received from the intensity of the Magician's gaze, that she would be a bird no longer, and how this hollowed her out before a single knife touched, or a single one of the Magician's creatures had burrowed into her flesh and curled up there. How she longed for the days spent in her cell in the underground prison, the nights spent sharing with the little foxes. How that was now some idyll, some pleasant memory of purgatory.

The children with their dead eyes had returned to crowd close, lustful for the demonstration. The Magician had made them lustful in that way, focused their energy and intent to mirror her own. They were a family, in their way.

"Isadora, you are so beautiful," the Old Man said, but she could not see his face there among the multitudes, nor Sanji's. She could not understand what he was saying, except that now the Magician was saying it.

"You are a lovely thing," the Magician said. "But you can be more beautiful still . . . and more useful."

"The seeds of me are the seeds of you," the Strange Bird said. Something Sanji had told her, whether in a dream or in the lab, she could not remember.

The Magician did not miss a beat. "Well, that may or may not be true, but you are the one undergoing transformation. Without an anesthetic, dear. But you are a made thing, as I am not, so you shouldn't need it. You will find ways to numb yourself. If you even understand me and aren't just running on a loop like a mechanical nightingale. But you must because I cannot do it for you."

"One by desert, one by sea. One by forest, one by marsh."
The labs. The research. Her, the bird.

"And one on the table, ready for the work," the Magician
replied.

By her look if not her words, the Strange Bird understood. It was a look Sanji had given her and others in the
lab. Before they added, subtracted, divided, multiplied, as
if there were a way, in referring to the math of it, the acts
became abstract, not about flesh and blood at all.

She would not be recovering from this. She would not
escape from the observatory, not, at least, as herself.

The pain hit sharp and piercing, as if each of the children
held a lit match and set each individual feather on fire, with
each quill turned into a blade driven into her flesh. And
still this could not describe the agony as the Magician took
her wings from her, broke her spine, removed her bones
one by one, but left her alive, writhing and formless on the
stone table, still able to see, and thus watching as the Magician casually threw away so many parts that were irre-
placeable. As she gasped through a slit of a mouth, her
beak removed as well.

While there came the rush and withdrawal of the wave
that was the roar of the children's approval and the bright,
tight leers of their compressed faces, eclipsing the heavens

above. The rapt silence with which they held their breath at some new trick the Magician had performed through reduction of the Strange Bird's flesh. So invasive and yet completed with such smooth and clinical assurance that the Strange Bird did not have the option of dying of shock, flayed as she was. Remade as she was.

"Every created animal," the Magician said in a vague, disconnected voice. "Every created animal, every single piece of biotech, has a signature, or sometimes many signatures. Of their creators. Of their intent. And these signatures leave a message, intended or not. And if you can read those messages, you can . . . oh, what have we here? Override and interlacing that should not be there—a second voice. Let me just take a moment to snuff out that voice.

"There. Done. Now, as I was saying, although I doubt anyone in this room can understand me, I certainly hope not, this 'surgery' would not be successful without translating the signatures. The intent. To reform intent, *you must not cut against the grain*. For example, this 'bird' actually contains traces of squid and even human influence. It also has a quite strong camouflage ability—so strong it invests in both physical camouflage and internal camouflage. So, what shall I change this creature into? Something of personal use to me. Can anyone guess? No, of course you can't. But soon enough most of you will be hopping up onto this table to find out for yourselves."

There came a moment, pulled at, reshaped, spread out flat, that the Strange Bird found a way to turn off the pain, made each thing taken remote from herself. The ceiling fell away and the laughter of the children and even the hands of the Magician, so complicit in dissolving her, and even the little, innocent creatures, like the spider and the worms, that the Magician had sent inside her on journeys to make the Magician's repurposing easier.

All of this fell away, and, in the end, there was only the head of the fox on the wall, staring benevolent down on her, shining with that blue, unfading, eternal light, that beatific agony, and the compass that still lived within her and pulsed in secret and had hidden itself from the Magician. It pulsed known to her alone and she could not scratch the itch, and yet the compass by its distraction, its presence, let her know she was still alive. Transformed from compass in her mind to a beacon, calling out to the southeast, to a place remote, communicating that she could not come there, but the southeast must come to her. And the pulse was the pulse of her mind, her heart, of the remnants that survived in what was left of her body. This was all that saved the Strange Bird, although she was bird no longer. The beacon that meant something other than flesh lived within her still.

Sanji, captor and confidante both: "There is no shame in going dark. There is no shame in giving up, for a time."

And the Old Man said, peering out from his corpse at the edge of the courtyard, "I live in darkness now. I live there. I die there. I live there."

She had no wings. She was spread out impossibly long and wide across the table. Hours and hours had passed. The children had lost interest and left. Only the fox and the Magician remained, and the fox had no choice.

The Magician wiped the sweat from her face, stared down at her new creation, which stared back up at her from eyes hidden among the iridescent feathers, gulped like a flounder through a mouth now hidden on the underside of what the Magician had created from her flesh.

"I will wear you as a cloak once you've recovered," the Magician said. "No one will see me approaching. I will be invisible wrapped in you, and for that I thank you, though I doubt you will enjoy it. But that is the price of change. Someone always pays."

The thing on the stone table lay still. The thing on the stone table had already taken on the texture and color of the stone table, as was its nature. The thing on the table listened to the pulse of the beacon and counted each beat, waiting.

Where was she headed?

What did she hope for?

Where did she wish to come to rest?

THE FOURTH DREAM

In the fourth dream, Sanji is a bird and she flies beside the Strange Bird high above the Earth, where no pain and no suffering can be seen or felt. Sanji as bird has an odd aspect, for her bird-flesh has been made from many different animals, some that can fly and some that cannot. Yet still she flies.

The Strange Bird is made of air, not of flesh at all. She relishes being made of air, revels in it, can soar invisible and triumphant. She wonders why Sanji would choose the guise of avian when she could be air, she could be nothing.

The Strange Bird lives in this dream for a long time. She lives in it for as long as she can.

TIME AND THE CLOAK

Unexpected, in the aftermath . . . that Charlie X adored her, ran rough fingers over the feather cloak when he thought the Magician wasn't looking, and by his touch the Strange Bird learned more of her own contours and reach, for there were parts of her that could not feel at all, were rendered numb, and by the distant ghost of Charlie X's hand she began to sense the map of her new body.

"Soft," Charlie X murmured, as if he had never known anything soft before. "Pretty." Admiring a handiwork not of his own doing. All he had done was kill and eat a human being. All he had done was pursue her, catch her, and bring her to someone even worse.

The Magician slit Charlie X's throat often, yet often he returned and each time the Magician had grown more used to him and relied on him more. The Strange Bird lost count of how many times Charlie X's throat had been cut, how many times the mice poured out. But each time, Charlie X's hand shook worse and the sadness in his eyes overtook the rest of his face.

The Strange Bird loathed his touch. What he gave her in awareness he took away a hundred times over in how she had no say in the matter. Now she was the Old Man in the trapdoor, half-in, half-out. Unmoored, circling around, circling back, unable to escape yet able to escape.

There was no true way for the Strange Bird to regain herself in the aftermath of atrocity. She had no wings. She had no wings, and the panic of that, the shock, was only tempered and made distant by how many of her senses the Magician had stripped from her. Her mouth could not sing but only breathe in shallow, uncomfortable gulps. Her eyes now saw only what was above her when the Magician laid her to rest at night and what was above her when the sun rose before the Magician took her up again.

Between, she did not have the comfort of true sleep, but only a half-awake imitation so that the Strange Bird always felt exhausted, forgot so many times that she had been mutilated, beat wings that were not there, and quivered instead, and quaked in her smooth, thin formlessness and for long moments did not know or forgot what manner of creature she had been turned into.

Somewhere in the horror of the first nights, the Magician, drunk with her power, gave the Strange Bird over to the feral children, and allowed them to run through the observatory holding her aloft as they had Charlie X. Their filthy hands all over her, pulling and prodding and trying to rip and sometimes to bite, and by all of this the Strange Bird knew that the Magician was using her children to test the strength of what she had made.

The children gave out a mighty cry and brought her up to the telescope and draped her over the broken eye and swung from the ends of her that dangled down. They yanked her from that spot and brought her to another and swung once again. They gnawed like Charlie X's mice, but not as gentle. They wrapped themselves six at a time in the length and width of her and the Magician laughed and pretended she could not see their legs and heads peeking out.

She saw again the storm of beetles and the real storm that had come up behind them, and she was both the beetles, ripped apart by the cyclone, and the storm billowing out senseless and raging. Even as from the outside the Strange Bird was utter stillness and silence.

Cloak and cowl both, draping and undraping, which hurt the most as she would again forget the lack of wings and feel unbalanced, experience vertigo and be unable to catch herself, and forever there was the sensation of being undone, of being only a skin slid across the skin of the Magician, and that this made her less than animal, less than nothing, a mere surface with no depth, a flat pool of water that would in time recede to even less than that.

"Such a brilliant cloak, such a useful cloak," the Magician said to the Strange Bird when she had retrieved her treasure from the children. "You will be witness to great things, important things."

The Strange Bird would be gasping inside, choking, unused to the cascade, the steep fall away. Caught herself, saved herself, only by imagining the cowl of herself around the Magician's face as her two true wings transformed and curved together around that lionesque head. That *she* chose to frame the Magician's features and that in any moment she willed, the Strange Bird could bring those wings apart, break the frame, bring the Magician visible. Or wrap the Magician's face so tight that she would suffocate.

To live in such closeness to the creature that had unmade her could not be described, made every moment tense. To be intimate enough to feel the Magician's heartbeat and the tensing of muscles in her taut back, the strength in those shoulders, the breath of the Magician sometimes upon the side of the cowl, those lithe fingers pulling at the fabric of her feathers and her life. There were the hands of the Magician upon her, worse than Charlie X's, to place her properly and the prickle and tensing as her feathers changed without her bidding to match whatever landscape they moved across.

THE MAGICIAN'S COMPASS

If the Strange Bird had a compass that compelled her, then the Magician, she came to understand, had a compass, too. This was a slow understanding, one that leaked into her over weeks, months, and years. For nothing came to her easily now or with any speed.

At true north lay the great bear Mord, the Magician's mortal enemy for control of the city. At true south lay the Company building, a place that the Strange Bird knew as a kind of laboratory on a scale far outstripping the one from which she had escaped. To the west, the Magician's regard for her transformed children, her observatory headquarters, while to the east, forever changing in the intensity with which the Magician regarded them, were a scavenger named Rachel and a competitor of the Magician's named Wick. Rachel worked with or for Wick and Wick made creatures much as the Magician did, and used them to barter for goods.

The Magician would meet Wick in secret near the observatory, slipping on the Strange Bird and then slipping out past her own sentries to admonish Wick or order Wick or try to exert influence. Wick was never amenable, always as slippery as the Magician, a thin, pale man whose affect was like being only a surface and not a creature.

"Remember how much I could hurt you," the Magician would say, and the Strange Bird would wonder why she did not hurt Wick then, there. Only in time did she realize Wick must himself be formidable, in his way, but by then the Strange Bird did not care because everything about her was falling apart, falling away.

But the Magician also spied on Wick, and Rachel, from a favorite spot—standing beside a swollen, polluted river below a cliff into which had been carved dwellings. Once, the Magician stood there for so long that the Strange Bird noticed, came out of her thoughts, for every muscle in the Magician's body was tense, on alert. Soon, as dusk fell, Rachel and then Wick came out onto the balcony above and began to argue. The Magician began to mutter and argue with herself, and this was how the Strange Bird knew, for the Magician could read lips and said the words out loud to better house them in her memory. The Strange Bird had no opinion of Wick, but she liked how Rachel held herself, compact and apart, and precise.

That same day, the Magician had undertaken the much more perilous watching of Mord. For under cover of the cloak, the Magician would draw near to Mord's filthy flank, even when he sat ponderous and huge and feasting on bloody remains; she would stand so close she could have touched him, her scent masked by the stench of blood, and even remain there, silent and vibrating with some secret need—for danger, for death?—as he rose, when another might have run, feared being crushed. But the Magician would just let out a shuddering breath that wracked her body.

The Magician became methodical about Mord, studied his habits as he grew ever larger and more unhinged. She would follow him back to the Company building he still defended and observe the fraught conversations between those within and the great bear without.

"It is falling apart," she might coo, triumphant, on her way back to the observatory from such missions. "He is grown too bloodthirsty, and they are failing. We must accelerate the process. We must make of everything a chaos. We must be the sign of order."

Mord held no interest for the Strange Bird now, so many months or years since she had first seen him. His flying felt more like mockery now and his brutality made him of a piece with the Magician. The impossibility of him could not inspire or impress, for so much that seemed impossible had already been wrought upon her. So she clung to the back of the Magician and experienced Mord only when the Magician walked away from him, and thus Mord was, to her, something large and incomprehensible that became smaller and smaller over time.

Always as the Magician went about her business, took up her positions, visited her haunts, always the Strange Bird must look the other way, stare out at whatever horizon the Magician had turned her back on, and often the Strange Bird hoped that she stared out at a future unfamiliar to the Magician. And that out of that horizon would come a threat, someone or something to kill her, and she did not care if they ripped the Magician's fine cloak apart to get to her. For she was no fool, even now, and knew her fate was bound up in the Magician's fate.

But by then, whenever this was, the Strange Bird did not want to live, or did not know she could live, and that was the same thing in the end.

THE ISLAND

Sometimes, in the early days of endless despair, the Strange Bird let the Old Man come to her, to crawl up the sand of the island that was her sanctuary, toward the tree. As the Magician pursued some mission or late at night when the bird cloak lay again on the stone table for a time, the Magician plotting or seeking counsel with a spy or underling, or, worst of all, hung in a closet in the dark in the Magician's secret living quarters deep beneath the observatory.

The Strange Bird would let the Old Man appear to

her and he would call her Isadora and he would call her beautiful, and his "beautiful" was different enough from the Magician's that for a moment she would find a false comfort and she would see the foxes on the dunes, looking down at the prison. But then she would see Charlie X pulling the Old Man into the ground or the Old Man confessing his secret and she would know the vision for what it was, weakness.

"Weakness can be a strength," Sanji told her, but the Strange Bird did not believe her. This form of weakness was a dissolution of the self, a rewriting of history.

Sanji spoke much more often now and the Strange Bird retreated when lost in her thoughts to the lab island of trees surrounded by the moat of crocodiles. Sanji would sit on a branch next to the Strange Bird's perch and they would talk.

The island was weakness, too, but although she never left her perch, never flew, on the island she had wings. Not the Magician's possession, not Isadora.

The Strange Bird pondered often the last changes the scientists had made to her before she escaped the lab, for better to think of those changes than the ones the Magician had made.

"I can guess, just as you can guess," Sanji replied, though the Strange Bird had not asked the question. "Maybe I gave you a map of the lab. Maybe I put a compass in your talons, wanted you to escape. Because I could not."

The Strange Bird didn't believe that. Sanji could have escaped at any time, like her companion.

"How? I had no wings."

Twinge of panic in the Strange Bird, fought the impulse to flap her wings there on her perch. Feared both that she would be able to and that being able to would unhinge her, drive her mad, and she would never return to that perch, or any perch. But float up into the sky and into the night until there was no scrap of her left.

Sanji: "You could fly over all that distress and disaster and contamination. You could fly over it and survive it and get somewhere better." Even as a phantom, Sanji said this too casually.

Was there somewhere better? Here, inside the dream? Sometimes Sanji had taken her to the lab garden, to the apple tree that grew there, but always after a session in the blood room, so that the gardens, for all their peace and comfort, were tinged red, and she could not even see them for the turmoil raging inside. How could Sanji take her to the garden then? How could Sanji not see what that did to her?

"But me?" Sanji said. "I was already lost. It was already too late for me. I had put too much of me into you. And I could not reach my companions—the satellites were gone. I had no choice but to trust in you."

By this, the Strange Bird realized that Sanji back at the

laboratory must be dead, and had been dead many months, or maybe longer, for time moved so differently for the Strange Bird now that she could not tell if she was having these made-up conversations scant hours after the Magician had transformed her, or many years later.

Here she had not even the clue of a slit of sunlight looking out on a dune. Here, she had only what she sought to push away: the number of operations the Magician had performed on her since her capture. Three or four? To make the cloak perfect. To make her perfect. Five or six or seven?

Perched there on the island, no longer bounded by four glass walls but only water that went on endless, like the world, the Strange Bird could sometimes pretend to know.

Sometimes, too, she would search the faces of the children who still crowded around the stone table during her operations—for some sign, not just of sympathy but remembrance, a spark in the eyes that said they had been witness to her mutilation, that someone besides the Magician still understood that once she had not been this rag of flesh.

She could not trust telling the time by the children, though, even as their features were transformed by the Magician's modifications, when they came to resemble Charlie X and were less like themselves. Because the truth was, the children came and went and they were never the same children or the same transformations and so this, too, was unreliable, only a way to keep track of how far along the Magician might be in her plans in the moment, and when she had suffered setbacks or was raging in her triumph.

What time was it? Time for the Magician to take her out of the closet and wear her into the world.

"You are the best of us," Sanji said. "You are better than all of us. I've made sure of it. I know the way is long and I know it will be dangerous and you will be afraid. But you must keep trying, must fly on."

The last thing Sanji had said to her back in the lab. The very last thing. The worst thing, before the intruders.

Be gone, the Strange Bird commanded Sanji, and the woman disappeared from the branch.

But the glowing blue fox head remained, suspended in midair, facing her.

The Strange Bird thought it odd the fox head never left that place, that it smiled at her with such ferocity and did not bend to her will. As if it were real and not just in her mind, and some days the puzzle of that was all she had left to cling to, in all of her confusion of time, lying exposed to the world so not herself, that she might as well not exist and thus wished that others did not exist.

Then it would be another morning or night and she would be the Magician's protection and secret and they would steal out into the city and on the worst or the best days everything would click into place and she would know the number of years it had been since she lost her wings and she would cry out silent and plead with the god the lab scientists had not believed in that she be able to go back to the place where she could not tell the time at all. The god that nonetheless the lab chaplain had invoked when consecrating the experiments, as if it made a difference to the Strange Bird. For what was anyone who would allow such a place if not a monster?

More years passed. She witnessed the rise of the Magician's army and how the Magician betrayed Charlie X, such that his mice could not save him and he died out in the wastelands, next to an old well, staring up at the sky, looking exposed that far from his trapdoor refuge. How the mice spilled out of Charlie X's throat in the end, and ran off into the long grass with such an exuberance and speed that she wondered what had bound them to Charlie X for so long, under such conditions.

She experienced the same terror as the Magician when the Company created Mord proxies: normal-sized bears in Mord's image, ones who could not fly but were vicious and preternaturally strong . . . and how little time it took the Magician to adjust. She saw how much the Magician loved and hated the remnants of the Company. She realized that the Magician would do anything to rule the city, take any risk. That she considered it her right and destiny. That the Magician was alone in that, no matter how many stood beside her.

By then, the Strange Bird's beacon had grown weaker and weaker, a thready pulse, and some days she would wake blind and only the Magician's constant needles, the release of foul liquids into her skin, would revive her. She had by then half forgotten what the beacon meant, or that it might once have been a compass leading her southeast.

Finally, there came the days when she gave up so much of herself, when she relaxed into nothing so perfectly that the comfort was too painful. As the pulse failed the knowledge of this thing existing within her, reminding her of a different life, was worse than if it had been pulled out of her by the Magician at the start.

THE BLUE FOX

And yet. Yet. Beyond the end of her story, of herself.

There came one day the patter of quick paws in her head.

A familiar scent and a calling out to her, to the beacon inside, which was embers now, slowly cooling. The island lay encased in winter ice and no trees grew there. The chessboard, not an ocean, surrounded the island, and the animals on the squares were frozen, even the crocodiles, and their expressions set in agony. She could not keep it straight. She could not conjure up Sanji. The Old Man and Charlie X crept up in the shadows on the far side of the island and she could not stop them.

Yet there came this distant *patter*, this scrabbling and digging and from above the blue fox head that still floated above the island smiled and looked down and gave her the light she could not give herself, as if the true sun. What new thing was this, or was it old? Clustered behind the fox's eyes she knew now peered down many foxes, some of them familiar from the dune outside the Old Man's prison.

The blue fox head spoke in yips and barks. They did not speak in what was recognizable as speech, but still she knew the meaning.

We cannot help you, but we can track you, if the beacon still burns, and it will stop pulsing if you die, and you are close to death.

With this message came a welter of images the Strange Bird had to pick through to understand—their struggle, their planning, how they had escaped the Company, how they had their own vision for the city and how the Magician was their enemy. It took time to piece this together.

Do you understand?

There, under the moonlight, imprisoned by the Old Man, the Strange Bird had let them into her mind, and they had never really left. They could track her, but not help her, and she did not care that they could not help her. No one could help her, but it was enough that they could track her. That if she held on, they would know where she traveled at all times. That if she consciously allowed them in, the signal would grow strong. That she must not die, that she must let them in.

Yes, she said. Yes, I understand, and realized her fondest memory, one of her only good memories, was the cheer and mischief of the foxes on the dunes so long ago.

The ice melted from the island and Charlie X and the Old Man receded and the chess squares with their terrible cargo became the ocean again and the blue fox head smiled down and warmed her tired and forgotten soul.

Now as the Magician went about her war, her task of conquering the city, the Strange Bird could feel the foxes beside her, shadowing. They were the creatures from the broken places. They were the insurgents that no one could see. They schemed in the desert and danced and yipped for the joy of it because they were free and no one saw that they meant their dance to be the city's dance and for the city to be free. That if they could not have a fierce joy in their struggle, then they were not truly free but governed by fear and doubt.

She took hope in this as the Magician fought the Mord armies, fell back, lost the observatory after an ill-fated offensive, retreated underground to make her child warriors more fearsome still. The alterations ever more vicious and ever more meaningless; Mord's army was all predator, and their instincts created no hesitation, and their bloodlust could not be contained, and their questing, snuffling progress through building after building, trying to root out the Magician's mutants, left no trace behind, because they ate the dead and cracked their marrowed bones.

The Magician became more isolated, alone, lonely. She became more paranoid. They moved quick and traveled light, and never spent a second night in the same place.

She spoke to the Strange Bird more often, unaware that the Strange Bird betrayed her now just by living.

"Their monster is out in the city, spreading havoc, but I will let Mord deal with him. Their monster is young and knows so little," and the Strange Bird understood she spoke of what she called "Wick's creation," Borne, the one Rachel had kept close, the creature that could change shape and size and made the Magician suspicious of even her most trusted lieutenants among the children. For now she put them through all sorts of tests before she would allow them close, and even at times hesitated before putting on her living cloak.

"Mord must tire. Mord must falter. I will bring him low just by outwaiting him," the Magician would say, and the Strange Bird knew from the puzzled tone that it was the Company that had taken away Mord's ability to fly, not the Magician, that his rage at being earthbound was directed at the wrong enemy.

"They'll never leave the Balcony Cliffs without a push," she would say, and the Strange Bird knew she worried at the redoubt created by Wick, so it was no surprise when she gave Wick up to Mord's army and they were flushed out.

"When this is over, I will rebuild the city in such splendor no one will recognize it from before. There will be trees and schools and libraries and grocery stores and all the ordinary things a city should have," the Magician said, and the Strange Bird would ignore her, for this was the speech she gave to her child army, the vision she laid out for them even while her head was full of dead worms and living spiders and more corpses than Charlie X had ever known.

The Strange Bird was just a filthy old rag by then, draped across the Magician's shoulders, but even as a rag there would be no convincing her of the Magician's grace or mercy.

The Magician left piles of skulls behind her and burned bodies, and the altered children that had once followed from an ecstatic bloodlust and killing joy obeyed out of a taut fear—and the Magician preferred it that way.

THE LAST DAYS

Then a thing happened that confused the Strange Bird, for despite the desperate hope brought to her by the foxes, she was faded and dull and worn, had been through too much, kept enduring beyond what any living being should have to endure. She could not see well or hear or smell. She had only the echo of voices in her head, and the hope that among those voices the foxes still spoke to her.

So the Strange Bird could only *feel* what happened from the steel intensity of the Magician's body, how one moment she was relaxed and the next she held herself stiff and still and must be sore from the way that her muscles were so rigid, her shoulders so set, and the injury at the core of her, the shock. Then the frantic flight, the running down stairs, through tunnels, the chill of the underground and not of the light. That she spoke to no one around her as she hurried, because there was no one to speak to, which must mean the children were gone, in hiding, or defeated, and every-where, surrounding her, the Mord proxies.

South they went after that, the beacon within told the Strange Bird. South and further south, so that she knew their destination must be the Company building, while the foxes pulled at the frayed edges, urging her to wake up, so the beacon would pulse more strongly. Even as her initial surge of hope had faded with her health and it was less and less a matter that concerned her, locked inside her own brain, and she drifted, drifted, expected that she might soon wash up on a hillside beside Charlie X and perhaps be glad of it.

Twice, as the Magician approached the Company

building, they fled Mord proxies, who meant to force them north and west and out of the city. The reek of them penetrated even to the Strange Bird with her failing senses, and just as they reeked they could smell even the faintest scent of the Magician, or so she thought, and so stopped to rub mud on her face and offal on her boots, to throw them off.

But still, somehow, they found her because she had a beacon on her back. They lunged out of the buried and burned places in the sand and thus at the Strange Bird who as passenger could do nothing but take the quick rending of their claws in ambush before the Magician startled away, injured but not fatally.

The slash of fangs that just missed the mark, but did not miss the Strange Bird. But what was being cleaved and torn to one who had been so utterly destroyed already?

In the lee of an abandoned facility, the purpose of which had been lost to time and the sands, the Magician rested, enraged—gasping for breath and cursing her bad luck. Ranting at how preternatural the bears' tracking skills had been, when it was the foxes that kept their aim true, left the clues that betrayed the Magician's position.

They had been chased by Mord's proxies the entire night and into the dawn and the Magician did not care her cloak was leaking blood into the sand, and what that might mean for her camouflage, but only to tend her bruised ribs, and the long, shallow gash across her back, which was a cut in the Strange Bird that had sliced right through.

"They think they have me," the Magician told the Strange Bird crushed between her back and the wall. "But no one knows the Company building like I do. Except Wick, and he's headed there, too. If he makes it, I'll shadow him and pick his pockets. If not, you and I can still gather ourselves, wait it out."

The Strange Bird had no response. She existed in a peculiar world where for hours she had seen and heard only secondhand, her senses shut down.

The foxes were her eyes and ears instead, and she heard the Magician say those words from the vantage of a fox sneaking close, saw through the fox's eyes. How the Magician was invisible and the cloak was invisible, but for a flickering blue flame across the top of the cowl that only they could see, that was the Strange Bird's beacon.

The flame she must keep alive. She had imagined it as red, as pulsing red, but it was blue, blue as the fox head on the Magician's wall.

Still the Magician pushed on, past her own exhaustion, past the exhaustion of her living cloak. She laid her own traps, doubled back, found ways to evade as if she knew she must be visible to some, until the Company building was less than an hour's travel ahead of them. The Strange Bird could feel the growing concern of the foxes, something ancient and brittle and deep that made her shiver and doubt whether she knew them at all.

While behind them lay a horizon too terrible for the Magician to look at, something that made the Magician gasp the one time she had turned back to gaze upon it. Something that the foxes did not want to show the Strange Bird, that she must strain her blurry vision to make out, and only in the end could tell that Mord fought something as monstrous as himself against the skyline.

"There is only what is ahead," the Magician told her traitorous cloak.

While the ghost of Charlie X stalked them both, and his surgical mice chittered to the Strange Bird their ridiculous complaints. About the repetition of their work and their years of devotion to their host, expecting, perhaps, that she might have sympathy having served the Magician for so long. But she did not.

In the darkness, Charlie X eventually receded and she understood the mice that spoke to her were not the ones she had known, and that the tunnels there teemed with life, even if she no longer had the dark, glittering net with which to capture the traces, bring them close.

Plunging into the depths of the Company building. Down, down, down while the Magician murmured reassurance meant only for herself and then silence, the foxes having left her, and there was only the dark and the wound cutting through the middle of her and the certain knowledge that she was done, could not go on, finally could not go on, and in the darkness there was only Sanji, or the ghost of Sanji, or the Strange Bird talking to herself, saying, "Now it is time to rest."

The last transmission to her from that underground world: a vision of a better place, a place that did not exist in the world, and she could see birds in flight frozen in that image, birds that she envied, for they had been captured at the exact moment when they would never have to obey anything but the air, the wind.

Then she was falling into the Company building. She was falling from the island perch into the sea below, because she had glimpsed for a moment, just one single instant, that the crocodiles were gone, that it was safe to fall, and the only thing left to her was to fall.

So she fell, limp and formless into the sea, and the sea wrapped itself around her in a comforting embrace, the most kindness she had ever known. To be nourished and yet to be weightless, to not be part of someone else or be seen through someone else's eyes. But just to be herself.

And it was painful because she knew that could not be true, that it was a trick.

She was just a surface. She was never the bird striking the glass but only the windowpane.

Time could not fix that.

THE FIFTH DREAM

The tree on the island had lost all of its leaves and the crocodiles were skeletons. She sat huddled in the dead tree and from the island spread out the desert in all its desolate glory, and half-buried there, as after a storm: all of the dead animals from the lab, motionless but for their eyes. The blue fox no longer shone from above. There was just a vague, limitless glare.

She had no wings now, as she stood beside the tree, which had withered away to almost nothing. She could not remember her wings anymore, and thus they had fallen away from her.

"We gave up luxuries before they were gone, because we knew they would be gone soon," Sanji told her, sitting there beside her. "We knew it would be harder if we waited until they became extinct. We knew we would never survive that. So we made do with less and less. Not just luxuries but so much more beside. We put more of ourselves into other things."

"Into me," the Strange Bird said.

"Yes, into you."

"You never showed me kindness or consideration."

"I showed you both."

"You were cruel."

"Imagine being confronted by the end of the world. Imagine having the person you cared about so distant at a time when you needed not just her but what she was working on. Imagine everything going dark and not being able to talk to that person, even as you held part of the key. Imagine struggling so desperately hard and long to put it right."

"What is the compass inside me?"

"A last chance. A last hope. A kind of song only you can sing. Hidden."

"Where was I meant to go?"

"You have already been there."

But they were no longer on the island. They were in the garden, beside the apple trees, walking through the tall grass, after a session in the blood room, and there was nothing left to say.

WHAT DID SHE HOPE FOR?

Monsters fought and the world was drenched in fire and rain. While she was trapped in a sack. Swinging upside down. In a trapdoor coffin with a little bat-faced man. Up a tree. Falling through the air. Falling through the darkness.

Strange Bird plunged into a rich sea, a thick, warm sea that wrapped itself around her, comforting, nourishing as she floated in its embrace. How good it felt, to be weightless, to not be worn, to not be part of someone else. For by this sensation she also knew the Magician must be cast out or dead.

Just to float and all around the glide and waft and drift of that . . . There were other creatures in the mire with her, languid in their passage, but they did not concern her. Embracing her were long, thin worms, and they did not concern her, either. Where their touch alighted, her flesh healed and reasserted itself. There was a trickling sound, as of water filling a tub, and she was steadily lifted higher as the water level rose.

Her mind was clear even if her senses were muffled, as if she had taken a long, peaceful sleep and woken up without an alarm to prompt her. But when had she ever set an alarm?

From above, a beam of sunlight and faces that stared down at her around the edges of the pond. Not cruel, but concerned. Not angry, but seeking to help. The faces of Rachel and Wick, and by this and the ceiling above, the Strange Bird knew that she was no longer in the Company building but in the Balcony Cliffs, in the stronghold of the enemies of her enemies.

Wick had cuts across his forehead and bloodshot eyes, a

translucent, gaunt quality to him. Rachel was grimy and had nicks and burns. Whatever they had endured had been harrowing. Whatever they had endured had just ended, and by this, too, the Strange Bird knew not much time had passed.

"What is this thing?" Rachel said, cloudy, coming to the Strange Bird as if from a great height, from a place impossibly remote.

"What isn't it?" Wick replied, turning from his scrutiny of the Strange Bird to stare at Rachel.

"Can it fly?" Rachel asked.

"It has no wings," Wick replied.

"Does it bite?"

"If it does, should we eat it?"

"Much worse to eat a bomb than a beacon, I think I have heard you say. Should we end it? Is it dangerous?"

"No. It isn't. It's just weary and wary and ill-used, like all of us. It is not . . . itself. It can never be itself again."

Wick smiled wryly, something passing between them that was ancient, older than the Strange Bird, and that she would never intuit but could only observe. Something being set aside or reclaimed. While Rachel's hand was on his shoulder, as if in support.

"Can you save it?" Rachel asked Wick. "Should you?" A cryptic expression. Perhaps she would decide a living cloak was not worth concerning themselves with. Perhaps they would discard her as she had been discarded before.

Wick was busy unfolding part of the Strange Bird that had become tangled, spreading her across the thick water of the healing pool. His touch did not concern her. How thoughtful that they had dimmed the lights above so that she might not be blinded, so that the comfortable glow reminded her of winter by a low warm fire. When had she ever known winter? Or a fireplace?

"It's salvage," Rachel said. "Not worth much now. Look at all the scars. That wound right through the middle. The feathers—lost their color, lost their sparkle. I took this thing out of that place even though it looked dead already. I don't know why."

Still Wick remained silent, staring down at the Strange Bird's one good eye, at the mess that was her now, considering, reading what the diagnostic worms told him as they wrapped the Strange Bird in their spell.

If you could have seen me as the dark wings did, the Strange Bird thought.

But Rachel must have thought the silence meant disinterest, for she turned away, said, "I can just put it outside to fend for itself. Or use it for scraps. It's not important now . . . if that is what you want to do."

A tremor, a tremble, there from Wick, of a secret emotion, a sympathy that did not allow him to look at Rachel as he said it. But also in her gaze toward him the look of a companion who knew her partner so well that they did not need words.

"Can you believe the Magician wore this poor creature?" Wick said, not answering Rachel. "She also *made* it, in a way." Wick had a look of awe and disgust on his face. "The Magician *made* this creature into a cloak. I recognize her sutures, her markers."

"What was it before?"

"A mix of things, but in outward form . . . a bird. A large bird with iridescent wings. A powerful bird, to make such a long cloak. No matter how the Magician butchered it."

"Outward form?"

"Too much human in it. Very complex. Nervous system modified. Can still see those places. Neurons redistributed, not just in what was the head, but in the *feathers*, which are a hybrid, contain cephalopod. That is why she can still think—her brains are all over her body. I don't know if the Magician knew that."

"*That* . . . is human?"

Wick nodded, hands were on the Strange Bird again. Soft, quiet hands, and where they touched her, information flowing into Wick through his fingers.

"What was it made to do before the Magician?"

Wick shrugged. "Only guesses. There could be more than one reason. But before the Magician got hold of her, this bird was a kind of . . . dispersal system for genetic material. It would have been reseeding the world as it flew. Microscopic organisms."

"But now?"

"The Magician snuffed that out, took away her wings, too. Took away her bones." Wick withdrew his hands from the Strange Bird. "The signature is much more than that. Sometime before the Magician altered her, someone modified her to add a lot more human functionality and decision making. Very specific. Normally, this would be distributed, pulled from multiple sources. This is one source. This transfer conveyed personality traits, too."

"I don't understand. Is that important?"

"Important? I don't know. Interesting, definitely. Whoever did this shortened their own lifespan to do so, or at least weakened themselves. As if it was more important part of them be in this new form."

Their silence, the weariness on their faces, was the Strange Bird's weariness, too. For the bloodshed, for the senseless acts in the name of order, the name of the city's resurrection.

She knew it took them an effort not just to discard her.

Inside the Strange Bird, the worms moved, binding up the wounded places, and with each moment the beacon became more of a compass again and the little foxes were receding, no longer needed or needing her, and she saw them again where they belonged, on the distant dunes, their smiling expressions in the slit of sunlight, the love that came from them for one another and for her and for their fallen comrade, the blue fox the Magician had nailed to the wall. So long gone in truth, and although the island had disappeared, she felt the loss, but only for a moment, and the worms were still making her strong and waking her up, returning what the Magician's spider had taken away, making stalwart what had been malleable, and she felt the urge to fly although she could not.

"You are strong," Sanji said in her head. "You have a compass within you. You will leave this place. You will survive it." And for the first time, the Strange Bird believed that it might be true, but not because Sanji had said it.

Wick was still talking and the Strange Bird listened with half an ear, understanding some things and not others. Wanting to know some things and not to know others.

"There's something else, too," Wick said. "A kind of genetic imperative, buried deep, tied to a location. This bird, this creature, would, for most of its life, have felt an overwhelming desire to reach that place, ever since the modifications that made it more human. And deep in that place, too, there is a message it has carried, encoded so I can't read it."

"Should we let it go, then?" A particular weight on this.

"Yes. Yes. After everything that . . . If we can. She can't

be fixed, not in the usual way. There are things gone forever and things I can't replace and things I don't understand. But I can stay true to what she was meant to be. I can strip away the conditioning. The coordinates will remain, but what I fashion out of this . . . this mess . . . will be able to choose for itself what it does, where it goes. This creature hasn't had that for a long time."

In the end, there were four from one, when Wick lifted the Strange Birds from the vat of his converted swimming pool, and the rest of what had been a living cloak sinking insensate to the bottom, there to be fed upon by the little fishes and the mudskippers and the things without fins that hid there and wished not to be found. To be sent into motion, to dance, in the darkness, by the sharp, quick kiss of teeth and the snap and tear so that the cloak seemed to dance for a time, to rise and fall as of its own volition but only, really, by the will of those who feasted upon it, and the dying cells did not mind, wandered where they would, passed from mouth to mouth and honored in their way.

The Strange Birds made their way to the balcony, two held by Rachel and two by Wick. They were finch-small, drab, but swift and clever, and each identical to the others and each believed they were the original, and each held every memory of the others. They stared at one another and saw themselves. Trilled out chirps that were coordinates and communication both, the secret code of all things. Their minds were the same as before, but quicksilver, darting.

The lightness of their bodies was a marvel for them, a celebration and a miracle. Dispensing with weight as if it, too, were a cumbersome cloak sinking to the bottom of the pool.

The hands that held them released them up into the air over the poison river at the same time, tossed them up with laughter and celebration, like benediction for that place, and up, up, up they flew out into the sky together, in delight, exulting in the feel of it, the sheer power of movement, doubled back to look as one upon the couple standing on the balcony, and then wheeling over the river, through the trees that lined it, and then south.

No longer the Strange Bird, but always the Strange Bird.

WHERE WAS SHE HEADED?

The ecstasy of flight, the ecstasy of choice, and three of the four chose where the compass pointed—southeast and southeast and southeast, singing the song of that imprinted in their heads. The fourth wanted no part of either compass or city, but only solitude, and struck out to the north, and the rest held that Strange Bird blameless and sang to her until she was just a dot on the horizon.

Then off the three went in earnest, buffeted by the air, unused to the lightness of their bodies after being so earthbound and heavy, and their flight at least in part to flee the memory, to escape from what had been so terrible to bear. Their bodies shining with the sunlight, their beaks bright, their eyes bright.

Over the city and out into the desert, beyond the ruined Company building and beyond the little foxes and beyond any reach of the Magician's ghost. Across the vast stretches they flew, with purpose, into and through blazing heat, like arrows shot to the heart of a target. On they sped. Alert, alert, alert. Avoid, avoid, avoid. Looping and dipping in their passage and twisting around together, dispersing, for flying after so long would forever be so new.

On the third day, their profile against the sky triggered an old missile system buried in the earth, which sent five tunneling into the air at their approach, in a widening trajectory like an opening hand, and although they banked, slowed, then flew faster and gained both altitude, they could not lose them, and one of their number peeled off and led the missiles up over the desert.

Remember me, but fly on, she told them as she pushed her body to aerial acrobatics no songbird had ever attempted. There came the explosion, feathers drifting down. Another soul extinguished. Would it ever end? It would never end as long as there was life on Earth.

But the two Strange Birds flew on, sang their unique song, which they knew now no other bird had ever sung, and still always and ever to the southeast, gaining on their destination, taking comfort in each other's company.

At a watering hole lined with palm trees, dipping down to drink at two of the four compass points: a long, low, sand-colored predator, stealthy, surprised them. But not quickly enough, and they rose up in a chatter and scolding, indignant, remembering the forbearance of the foxes.

They pushed on through the dark rather than stay in that place, out of caution, and for a long time they flew without rest or water, for they could feel that they were close and wanted no delay. The compass beat fit to burst in both of them and it rang in their ears, made them see stars with the extravagance and boldness of it, but it also gave them the energy to continue on, dropping mass as they went, using up all of their muscle so that they might experience the brilliance of dawn at altitude, breaking through fog and clouds, with marauders below who saw them and shot at them, but could not find them with their wayward ammunition, and evading any creature seen flying toward them out of the limitless blue.

Three days out from the source, the sound of the wind changed, and they could smell the sea salt even that far from the water, and it drove them harder, but they lost all caution in their joy, and did not notice the shift in the sound coming to them, or the way the breeze thickened and came upon them with predatory intent.

A falcon screamed down from above and speared one of the two, and peeled off to rise again before the survivor had time to evade or mourn the loss, as if there had always been one and not two. As if there had always only ever been one Strange Bird. But from above, even dying, the companion defiant, urging the last on, and blessing the bird that had caught her, for it was only acting as to its nature and there was no cruelty in that.

The Strange Bird flew on alone, sobered, through storms and night and the cold. Ignored the hint of dark wings far above, ignored everything but the compass that beat like a second heart as she neared the ocean, and in that heart she could sense the pulse of the lost ones, all of the lost ones, from the lab, from the prison, from the Magician's war.

There need be only one. Only one need fly on, make it all the way to the end, wherever the end might take her.

WHERE DID SHE WISH TO COME TO REST?

On the tenth day, the desert ended and the dark blue remnants of a vast ocean in retreat leapt up into the Strange Bird's vision. The ancient waves, the curling salted lip of the bay and the beaches extending so far outward, strewn with rocks and seaweed . . . she had never seen anything like it before except in her dreams. Water had always been what came out of a bottle in the cage or the tepid moat surrounding the island. But the ocean felt new and exciting, despite being so old, and the brisk wind brought the smell of driftwood and barnacles, the almost spicy but fresh scent of the tidal pools, the funk of the things that had washed up.

She perched within the safety of a dense, stickery bush on the edge of it all and let the wind seek her out between the branches. The city was so far distant, she did not know if she could ever find her way back to it, and this, too, was comfort.

In the crook of a branch, surrounded by thorns, the Strange Bird slept that night, soothed by the rush and withdrawal of the waves and the sea salt, the seeking, willful breeze that tugged at her.

The first dreamless night. The first night of full sleep that she could remember, without interruption or panic. Such an ordinary thing, and yet such a mercy.

Down the coast, then, in the early morning, with the fog come rolling in off the sea, always south, following the line of the surf. Down and down, in such a small form that now she could take time to marvel at how different it felt than before, what she remembered of being as big as the dark wings. She liked the feeling of being winnowed down, as if there had been too much of her before, that anything unnecessary had been taken away and what was left was pure.

Speeding through the remains of old coastal orchards, where the splash of red or orange reminded her of Sanji and the apples, or the garden. These gnarled trees driven low and complicated by the constant wind and erosion, and the rich smell of wildflowers, which grew deep and thick and which she flew through to feel the tickle of their petals against her legs.

While on outcroppings of black rock slippery, flopping animals called out liquid barks and let themselves fall into the sea, submerge, only to reappear, all dark whiskers and large, sad eyes. And farther out sea monsters such as she could not fathom made themselves known by their vast shadows against the deep blue of the water.

The second night, she found herself in a place where the sea cliffs grew tall and the land again became more desolate. She found an alcove in the weathered stone, stinking of seaweed, and slept with one eye open for weasel and rat, for all of those natural and most unnatural of predators. But most of all for humans. To go for days now without seeing a person was a blessing for her, and calmed her thoughts.

She was not afraid in this, but bold, for what could happen to her but that she should die, and she had already died so many times.

On the third day, in the morning, she took shelter during a sudden squall and then emerged to the sun glistening off the tops of the whispering waves, took flight. Soon enough, the compass in the Strange Bird pulsed wildly. She had just risen above a hill, come close to the cliff face, and then leveled out low across the grass atop that plateau, and there, ahead, perched on the edge of the cliffs, a ruined laboratory station, an apple tree growing beside it. Twin to the lab from which she had escaped.

Was this to be her destination? Something within her rebelled at the sight. To come all this way, to have endured so much, only to, in a sense, return to where she had started. Was there another island within? Another blood room and a garden? Despite the evidence, might Sanji's partner still live? She did not believe so. Nothing her dark net of senses told her brought back evidence of life.

She passed over once, twice. A great fire burn had washed black across the roof and swept antennae and other equipment with it. Some attack in the side of the building had split it open, and a tangle of desks and chairs and stainless steel tables had tumbled out, and bones, covered in moss and ivy.

The desert encroached close by—the lab existed on the

thinnest strip of green between land and water. Precarious and always under threat, but she could find no other human signs of life. Whoever had split open the lab had moved on, gone out to sea or traveled up the coast. Would they come back? Nowhere the Strange Bird knew of could be assured of a threat not returning.

The Strange Bird would not enter that building, fly through those narrow halls. She could not, it was too much, and she blessed Wick's gift to her, that she might *choose* to come to this place and then choose to leave it should she wish. Whatever the compass had been for, whatever Sanji had intended, the Strange Bird was too late.

There was a fatigue in that, a weariness, because she had come so far. There was also relief. To relinquish this traveling, to give up the quest, and to live a life, for as long as she was able. She did not even mind being alone now, for all that she had once hoped to find others of her kind. She knew they could not live within, for if they were indeed her kind, they would have rebelled against such a place, and have escaped long ago, or died trying.

Yet still the compass pulsed strong, when she had expected it would cut off now that she had reached the destination. So she followed it the last little way, away from the lab, toward the sea, even if it led her astray, for what was the cost?

Freshwater trickled from a stream nearby, ending in a

cascade over the cliffs into the ocean. In the mossy areas beneath the arc of water she sensed shelter aplenty, including a small cave. The compass within pulsed so strong she could hardly fly for the buffeting that came from within, but she ducked under the waterfall and into the cave. Within was a copse of dark green trees with purple berries she could smell were edible.

The compass stopped, and beat no more, for it lived not in proximity to its twin.

There, facing her on one of the trees, was a mirror reflection of her old self, the bird of many colors, the iridescent splendor, all of it. The old her, the beautiful her, the one with no experience. There in front of her, staring curious at this little bird that had snuck in the front door. But the Strange Bird knew who else lived within that mind, just as she knew what lived within her.

For a moment, both were silent, both cautious and wary. They stared. Until, slowly, the Strange Bird saw recognition, some trigger, and a wall broke down and neither could hide from the other.

"I wish this had been a better world, Sanji. I wish we could all have been better people. I wish I was still alive here to greet you. I wish our plans had gone better. I wish we could have saved the world. I wish, I wish . . . but even if you receive this message, I know it isn't true, that we failed. It was too late. I held on as long as I could, but . . ."

And the reply: *"I could not be with you, my love. But I can watch over you all my days."*

Everyone who had created the Strange Bird or interfered with her or had hopes or fears that had been placed upon her, or wished her ill, was dead. All of them were dead, and their plans with them. But the Strange Bird could see the future. They would rummage for food in the underbrush and alight upon the roof of the ruined lab, and hop over to peck at the windfall apples from the tree. They would make their nests and take their shelter against the cliffs, and they would live long, long lives. There upon the sea oats and bramble by the vast sea, with her companion or without.

All the senseless things. All the senseless and unimportant things that fell away from the Strange Bird in that moment, that were forgotten or became meaningless. It had been a human need, the compass pulsing at her heart, and she was, in the end, much diminished for having followed it.

Yet what did it matter. For what are bodies? Where do they end and where do they begin? And why must they be constant? Why must they be strong? So much was leaving her, but of the winnowing, the Strange Bird sang for joy. She sang for joy. Not because she had not suffered or been reduced. But because she was finally free and the world could not be saved, but nor would it be destroyed.

And the beautiful bird broke into song, and although it

was not a song any bird would recognize, the Strange Bird could understand it and whatever remained of Sanji inside of her recognized it and responded, and the two birds sang one to the other, the dead communicating to the dead in that intimate language.

ACKNOWLEDGMENTS

Thanks to Sean McDonald for his many kindnesses and everyone at MCD/FSG for being so wonderful—including Maya Binyam, Naomi Huffman, Katie Hurley, Jane Elias, Lenni Wolff, and Justine Gardner. I would also like to thank publicist Alyson Sinclair for being tireless and amazing, as well as my agent, Sally Harding, for also being tireless and amazing. All of these people are, as they say, good eggs.

The strange bird has been with me for many years and is intensely personal, so I am happy that two even stranger birds—and old friends—Matthew Cheney and Eric Schaller, read it in manuscript and offered many useful comments. Thanks also to Greg Bossert, Gwynne Lim, Christine Skolnick, Jeremy Zerfoss, and several others for their comments on early drafts. As with *The Southern Reach Trilogy*, I will give a percentage of any royalties I receive from *The Strange Bird* to environmental charities.